1 MONTH OF
FREE
READING

at

www.ForgottenBooks.com

By purchasing this book you are eligible for one month membership to ForgottenBooks.com, giving you unlimited access to our entire collection of over 700,000 titles via our web site and mobile apps.

To claim your free month visit:
www.forgottenbooks.com/free717137

ISBN 978-0-483-28771-6
PIBN 10717137

FORGET-ME-NOTS.

BY

JULIA KAVANAGH,

AUTHOR OF "NATHALIE," &c.

"O world! so few the years we live,
Would that the life which thou dost give
Were life indeed!
Alas! thy sorrows fall so fast,
Our happiest hour is when at last
The soul is freed."

LONGFELLOW.

IN THREE VOLUMES.

VOL. II.

FIDE·ET·FIDUCIA

LONDON:

RICHARD BENTLEY & SON.

1878.

CONTENTS

OF

THE SECOND VOLUME.

———

Phyllis and Corydon.

THE world was very full of handsome shepherds and lovely shep-
herdesses a hundred years ago.
You found them in books, in
pictures, in china—everywhere, indeed,
except in fair pasture lands or on the
slopes of grassy hills. Of the coarse
beings who wore the skins of Alpine
goats and the plaids of Scottish High-
landers ; who tended sheep through snow
or hailstorm ; who thought more of a well-
filled flask than of pastoral curds ; the
world took no account. They were made

for toil and pains and wrinkles and old age; whereas Corydon and Phyllis, ever blooming, ever young, fulfilled their lot if they charmed tender hearts and captivated wayward fancies.

Thus they had it all their own way in the world at large, but in France most especially; in no place more so than in the old castle of Saint Brice. What had brought this Arcadian pair to a rude stone keep, once the home of mailed men and mediæval ladies, and which still frowned above the Atlantic grim and defiant, though the days of chivalry had so long gone by? What had these pseudo children of smiling Greece to do in a land of barren heath, and in a home reared amongst rocks, at the foot of which the mighty waves came beating up all foam and fury, and whence they rolled back to their vast bed with a sullen, conquered roar? Vain questions. Madame de Saint Brice, a young widow smitten with the pastoral mania of her age, had willed it so, and brought them all the way from Paris in a volume indited by the Chevalier de Florian himself. Thus do we find her on a lovely summer morning dressing in her room for the rehearsal of a play in which she was to act Estelle to the Marquis de la Faille's Némorin. He was a widower, an admirer; and the Countess who longed to be turned into a Marchioness, took unusual pains in adorning her pretty person. She wore a blue taffetas petticoat, short and full, a low pink-laced bodice, clocked stockings, and high-heeled shoes; and on the top of her powdered head was perched a little straw hat wreathed with roses. "Madame la Comtesse looks lovely," said her handmaid Justine.

The Countess thought so too, but was going to utter a modest "Nonsense," when with a scream she exclaimed : "My crook ! where is my crook ?"

Justine, scarcely less alarmed than her mistress, looked for the crook, a gilt one adorned with blue ribbons, but it had vanished from the corner where it should have been standing. Mistress and maid

exchanged looks of dismay: the young
Count must have purloined his mother's
crook. Downstairs flew the Countess in
an agony of fear, wings would not have
been more nimble than were her little feet
as her high heels clacked down the stone
steps worn down by generations of feudal
ladies.   Panting and breathless, she
rushed into a low, gaunt room—all the
rooms were gaunt at Saint Brice—and
there found the young Count in his un-
dress jacket and shirt-sleeves, and in the
very act of poising the crook, previous to
hurling it, javelin-wise, through the window at an imaginary besieger in the moat
below. The Countess snatched the crook
from his hand.

" You naughty boy !" she cried ; " how
dare you !—and why are you not dressed ?"

The Count of Saint Brice was a handsome lad, with a brown face and rich black
flowing hair ; but he was also a haughty
young Celt, stubborn and proud, and his
lip curled as he answered,

" I will not dress for Corydon. He is
a peasant."

" Then how can Madame be Estelle if there is no Corydon to call Némorin when her lamb is drowning ? " asked Justine, who was settling the rumpled ribbons around the crook.

" Let the lamb be drowned," was the young Count's cruel reply.

" But, my darling," urged the Countess, " you are to be Corydon to the Marquis's little girl Phyllis——"

" I hate little girls," he interrupted.

Justine uttered a scream. " Oh ! If Monsieur le Comte had only seen this Phyllis "—whose real name was Madeleine —" this angel with golden hair and blue eyes, by whose side he, the Count, would look so handsome in his pea-green coat ! "

But flattery and entreaties proved vain. Count Philip de Saint Brice stood before the two women, handsome, bold, and defiant, with a stubborn " I will not be Corydon," in answer to all they could urge.

" The pastoral is done for," said the Countess, bursting into tears ; " and—and the Marquis will never forgive me."

The Count was a spoiled, disobedient son, but he was a loving one. He could not resist his mother's grief. He threw his arms around her neck, promised to be Corydon, and offered to dress at once.

" And you will not be rude to Phyllis ?" said the Countess, taking advantage of his relenting mood.

" No, no," he magnanimously replied; " I shall not."

The Marquis de la Faille lived in a pleasant inland château, with gardens around it that were the Versailles of the province. As they alighted from their stately old carriage, the Countess, pointing to a vista of white statues, shining fountains, and clipped trees, said softly : " Philip this is beautiful."

" I like the old moat of Saint Brice ten times better," stoutly answered Philip.

" Hush ! here is the Marquis. Ah ! how well he looks dressed as Némorin !"

It is not usual to dress for rehearsals, but neither the Countess nor her bosom friend, Madame de Mersan, who was to

be Eglé, nor the Marquis, nor any of the
other people who were to act in the
pastoral, would have cared a rush for it,
without the dressing. So Némorin, when
he appeared at the head of the perron to
greet his guests, was in the full bloom of
a peach-coloured coat of true shepherd
cut, and of a dainty straw hat and ribbons
all fresh from Arcadia. He was a fine
man, with pale blue eyes and a weak
nether-lip, but a very handsome, courtly
gentleman withal, though scarcely youthful enough for the part he had chosen.
The young Count eyed him with the cool
contempt of his coming manhood for a
disguise so effeminate, and crossed a noble
hall and splendid salons with the same
silent scorn of all he saw, till his mother
said gaily :

"Now, Corydon, here is Phyllis."

Corydon's haughty young eyes fell on a
little girl who might be some seven years
old or so. She wore a rich white silk
petticoat, and a little red velvet bodice
laced with blue. A cloud of golden curls

fell around her face and slender neck. Her blue eyes were bright as stars, her skin was the whitest Corydon had ever seen; a little black mole, not far from her dimpled chin, made it seem still whiter. When he gazed on this fairy-like being, the young Count felt bewildered and be- witched, not so much with her beauty, though she was very pretty, but because he had never before seen so dainty a little creature. He stared at her in silent ad- miration, and had eyes for nothing else.

The stage had been erected in a green- house; a few tall shrubs did very well for a bower in the foreground; a real lamb, alive, of course, was to be nearly drowned in a real river which flowed through banks of real grass, and on one of these banks Phyllis was told to sit whilst Corydon, nothing loth, stretched himself at her feet and handed her buttercups and daisies, which her nimble little hands wreathed into garlands. All the characters sustained their parts admirably, with one exception : the lamb bleated at the wrong times, and, unlike the man in the story, would not be drowned in the last act, but had to be pulled by his rose-coloured leash and pushed into a river three inches deep.

But all this was nothing to Corydon and Phyllis, with whom alone we have any concern. This being a rehearsal, they were allowed to talk, and Corydon was prompt to use the privilege.

"What little feet you have got!" he said, looking curiously at the two red leather shoes on the grass by him. "Can you really walk with them?"

"No," replied Phyllis, with a toss of her golden curls; "I do not walk—I run."

There was a pause. Then the boy's lean finger suddenly alighted on the black mole near Phyllis's chin.

"How pretty!" he said, admiringly; "is it real?"

"Do not be rude," said Phyllis, tartly, "and give me the buttercups."

There is no knowing how much more Corydon might have said, and Phyllis answered, in this strain, but for a person

whom history has called The Severe Aunt.
This lady held the whole pastoral in jealous contempt, and though intent on
watching Estelle and Némorin, she found
some spare vigilance to bestow on the two
children. Buttercups and daisies, little
feet, and real moles, indeed! At their
time of life, too! So first raising her
shaggy eyebrows in amazement, then
knitting them in wrath, this lady dragon
silenced the young pair with a loud
" Hush!" Corydon, who cared naught for
dragons, looked defiant; but little Phyllis
was frightened, and when the first act
was over, and the severe aunt's eye
averted, she took Corydon's hand and
stole away with him unperceived.

That first act was a great success, and
Eglé, Madame de Saint Brice's devoted
friend, was in rapture with Estelle's acting and good looks. As for Némorin, she
declared anyone could see he was smitten.
And these dear children! Nature had
surely intended them for each other!
Almost in the same strain did this amiable

Eglé address the severe aunt. That lady
was in her darkest mood : was not her
brother-in-law making a fool of himself—
and at his time of life too—before her very
eyes ? So when Eglé's soft, flattering voice
began commenting, in her ear, on his
good looks, fine acting, and so forth, the
severe aunt, turning on the speaker, said
sharply : " The man that marries more
than once is a fool."

Eglé shook her head and really feared
he was.

" And the woman who marries more
than once," began the severe aunt—

" Oh ! she is a monster," blandly interrupted Eglé, who was a very handsome
widow.

" I say she ought to be whipped !" exclaimed the severe aunt.

Slave-owners, it was said, used to like
to whip their slaves now and then ; so
even a figurative whipping may have its
enjoyments for some minds. The severe
aunt certainly looked at Madame de Saint
Brice's plump, white shoulders as if the

imaginary rod she was laying across them were pleasant to wield, and, thanks to the satisfaction this harmless rod gave her, Phyllis and Corydon were forgotten.

Happy children! They strayed to the garden between the acts. They ate cherries and cakes. They played, they ran, they sang; their friendship ripening faster than fruit was ever ripened by tropical sun—ripened so fast, indeed, that when the moment for parting came, Phyllis clung to Corydon, and, spite the frowns of the severe aunt, wept and begged that he would not go.

"My dear heart," said Corydon, "I must go, but—" a kiss on the black mole came in here and struck the severe aunt speechless—"I shall soon come again; do not cry."

Here the Marquis interfered, and by promising this tearful Phyllis to take her to see Corydon the next day, he induced her to let the youth free. Happy Madame de Saint Brice drove away beaming. Philip would marry little Phyllis, of course, and she would marry Phyllis's father, and the golden age had all come back.

The Marquis de la Faille was true to his word. He called on the Countess the very next day, with his sister-in-law and his little daughter. Phyllis at once stole away with Corydon, who put her on his back, and carried her up a steep stone staircase, dark and narrow, to an upper chamber, whence there was a grand view of the rock-bound coast and the foaming Atlantic.

"Would you like to live here?" asked Corydon.

Phyllis shook her head, and uttered a very candid "No."

"What, not live here with me!" exclaimed Corydon, frowning.

"Me" is an irresistible argument with some tender feminine hearts, even at that early age of seven, for Phyllis, suddenly altering her mind, declared, with delightful inconsistency, that she should like it of all things—with Corydon.

"And when you are tall enough," kindly said Corydon, surveying her little figure, "I shall marry you."

"And when we are married, you will carry me on your back as much as I like?" suggested Phyllis, insinuatingly.

Corydon surveyed her little figure again. "I daresay you will never be very heavy," he observed, meditatively; "besides, I cannot marry you just yet, you know. I must fight the King's enemies first. Perhaps I may get both my legs shot under me, like the Count of Boufflers who was killed at Fontenoy, when he was ten years old. He was charging at the head of his own regiment."

Phyllis knew nothing of the kind, but on hearing this piteous story, surely one of the most piteous of those days, she burst into tears, and sobbingly entreated Corydon not to be shot, and not to die. Corydon was already too much of a man not to like to make Phyllis miserable about him, so he only replied, "that he should see," until moved by her grief, he relented, bade her not cry, and comforted her with a kiss, and a lump of sugar-candy which he drew forth from his pocket.

Whilst this young shepherdess and her swain went on with precocious but harmless love-making upstairs, a storm, of which they were the innocent cause, was raging below. In her anxiety to keep watch on her brother-in-law, the severe aunt had neglected to see what became of her niece, but suddenly missing her, she exclaimed :

" My niece ! Where is my niece ?"

For this lady was one of those persons to whom the possessive pronoun is dear. Némorin had just been whispering some soft nonsense in Estelle's little foolish pink ear; her silly heart was elated, and she replied with much sprightliness, " And where should Phyllis be, save with Corydon ?"

" Madame," said the severe aunt, who hated a joke, " I say, where is my niece ?"

" And I say, where should Phyllis be, save with Corydon ?" retorted the Countess, who was bent on being witty.

The Marquis saw that a battle was imminent. He was an arrant coward, and went to a window, whence he gazed down with profound interest on the dull green moat below. But this neutrality availed him not. The severe aunt carried on the war with such spirit and vigour that in five minutes time she had prostrated her poor little enemy with this home-thrust, which also reached the Marquis in the window :

" Madame, you may Némorin and make a fool of my brother-in-law, but your son shall not Phyllis and make a fool of my niece."

Madame de Saint Brice burst into tears, the Marquis looked foolish, and the door of the salon flew open. Little Phyllis, red as a rose, her bright locks streaming behind her, rushed in, full of glee, " Do not tell him," she cried ; " do not tell him I am here," and she crouched behind a huge arm-chair.

In a moment the severe aunt, swift as a falcon, pounced upon this silly little dove and bore her away in her talons, not without enduring some protests in the way of kicking from Phyllis's little red-shoed feet. With a hasty excuse, the Marquis followed, to see, no doubt, that his little daughter did not inflict any injury on his respected relative ; and when Corydon entered the room in full cry, with a " I know you are here : I see you," he saw not Phyllis, who had vanished, but his mother in hysterics, and her friend Eglé administering salts and consolations in equal and alternate doses.

" My dear creature," she said, " I will make all right !"

" How can you ?" sobbed poor Estelle.

"My dear creature, it is the easiest thing in the world."

And the easiest thing in the world it was, after a fashion, to Madame de Mersan, for to comfort her friend, to soothe the severe aunt, and to save the Marquis from all further troubles of that kind, she married him before a month was over.

Little Madame de Saint Brice died five years after this, declaring that the treachery of her friend had broken her heart. As to the severe aunt, she goes out of the story of Phyllis and Corydon after the wedding-day, but there is no reason to believe that it extinguished her altogether. Indeed, it was an event which brought happiness to none.

Six months after his marriage the Marquis fled to his regiment, in the bosom of which he prudently remained. His wife went to Versailles, where she led a gay life, till having quarrelled with a Princess of the Blood, she was ordered back to Brittany, there to remain during His Majesty's pleasure. The lady had a high spirit. She would not vent her displeasure upon her husband, the Princess, or the King, but she would break in Phyllis. It may be that the child was not easily broken in; perhaps, too, there were too many inconvenient witnesses in the château; for her step-mother soon found that the best means of accomplishing her object was to send Phyllis to her own widowed sister, a Madame du Mésnil, who lived in the neighbouring seaport town. So judgment was held, sentence was passed, and Phyllis was banished from her father's house.

Madame du Mésnil lived close to the harbour, in a gaunt old mansion with tall windows and a nail-studded, oaken door. The aged servant-woman who brought Phyllis to this house, on a summer evening, raised the heavy knocker and let it fall again with a dull sound. A childish face, which looked very bright and rosy in the light of the setting sun, appeared at once behind the cross grating of a window on the ground-floor, and, in a clear, treble voice, this young janitress asked to know what the strangers wanted. When the woman declared their business, the little keeper of the place said, sententiously: " The little girl may come in, but you must not."

The servant tossed her head. She did not want to come in—not she: nor, to do her justice, did she make the attempt; and when the great wooden den was unbarred and unlocked from within, she just thrust in poor Phyllis, and walked away.

The little girl of the house was very pretty; she was also younger and shorter than Phyllis, though she was oddly dressed in a faded blue-silk sacque much too long for her, and wore a huge lace cap—quite big enough for a woman—on the top of her little fair-haired head.

" Come this way," she said, after sur-veying Phyllis from top to toe; and she clattered up a dark, old staircase, making a great noise with her shoe-heels, which were prodigiously high.

" What is your name?" she said to Phyllis, as they entered together a very dingy, old salon; then, without waiting for an answer, " My name is Manon. How old are you? I am thirteen. Stand by me and let us see in the glass which is the taller of the two," continued this little lady, leading her companion to a dull old mirror, and rising on tip-toe to survey her own image. It was a very lovely image, though so oddly attired, and the bright young face beneath the cap bore some resemblance to Phyllis's sad, childish countenance—such resemblance as one may find between the radiant sun and its pale sister the moon.

"I am the taller of the two," said Manon. "The heels of my shoes have nothing to do with it," she sharply added, detecting the look Phyllis cast at her feet. Then, in the same breath, she informed her visitor that she would have to give up her fine clothes: "for you will have to sweep the floors and wash the dishes, you know," she added, raising her young eye-brows. "But I shall let you sleep in my bed. Come and look at my room."

Obedient Phyllis went. Manon's room was like the salon, like the whole house— dingy and faded ; the hangings were moth-eaten, the blue lampas bed-curtains had lost almost every vestige of colour, the furniture was so old that it seemed ready to crumble to pieces. Everything looked so dull and so dreary in the dim twilight that Phyllis began to feel afraid. Was she alone with Manon in that great house?

"What about it?" answered Manon; "her mother and her two big sisters, Jeanne and Marie, were only gone to the play with the Viscount and the Marquis. They were Gardes du Pavillon, you know, and she, Manon, would go to the play too, a year hence."

Then began a glowing account of all the delights which the town afforded, in the way of plays, balls, and masquerades; and the Gardes du Pavillon figured so often in these narratives that Phyllis, wondering, asked who these gentlemen were.

"They are naval officers, you know," said Manon; "they are all nobles, all young, all handsome, and oh! they are so wicked!" she added, raising her eyebrows again.

"How so?" asked Phyllis beneath her breath.

"Why they spread nets at night in the streets to catch the girls, you know," said

Manon, "and they take them to the King's ships and sail away with them; and when they owe a good deal of money, they catch their creditors and carry them off to India and never pay them!" added Manon, triumphantly. "Then, when they have a fancy to it, they turn every one out of the theatre and keep the house to themselves. Oh, they are so wicked! But we need not be afraid; we are nobles, and they only catch tradesmen's daughters, you know."

Phyllis drew little comfort from this assurance, and timorously asked to go to bed. Perhaps she thought the terrible Gardes du Pavillon could not find her under the bed-clothes if they should take a fancy to invade the house. Manon let her creep into the big old bed, but kept her awake by talking of balls, Gardes du Pavillon, and a pink satin robe belonging to her elder sister which that young lady had promised to give her at some future period of time. 'Spite Manon's chatter and her own fears, Phyllis at length fell asleep, but towards dawn a great noise in the street below woke her. She heard a clash of swords, a woman's shriek, then all was still. Hiding her head under the quilt, she shook with fear, whilst Manon slept and dreamed of pink satin.

Even if Manon's stories had been false, Phyllis would have believed every word of them; but it so happened that they were true—tragic stories that still live in the records of those evil days, and which received the most tragic of all endings in the scaffold of ninety-three. Men were turned out with contumely from the theatre of Brest because the blood in their veins was not blue; the accounts of noble debtors were settled by luring plebeian creditors on board the King's ships and carrying them off to sea, and nets were spread in the streets of the city for girls and women who were not of the patrician race.

To that favoured race, though much fallen in substance, and still more in honour, Madame du Mésnil belonged.

She had beautiful daughters, and made the most of them. The young ladies were much admired by Messieurs les Gardes du Pavillon, and admiration sometimes took the shape of wine, sometimes it appeared as so many yards of velvet and satin. Nay, a turkey and a quarter of lamb often expressed the power of Jeanne's bright eyes and of Marie's smiles. Money was probably a rare offering, for Madame's last servant had left because her wages had not been paid for two years, and it was to supply her place and get her spirit properly broken that Phyllis had been placed under this good lady's care.

A hard life Phyllis had of it now. Manon was kind to her in a capricious sort of way, and kept her awake at nights talking of her future triumphs; but every one else was harsh and scornful to Phyllis. She was clothed in coarse grey camlet, to begin with, and made to do all the dirty work of the house. Nay, to her great terror, she had to go out on errands in the city and out of it, to get dainties for

Madame du Mésnil and her daughters, who were fond of good things. Thus, one bleak morning in autumn Phyllis was bid to go and get these ladies some fresh watercresses from a little spring which flowed through a farm outside the town. "And if you cannot get any, why, you need not come back," said Madame du Mésnil from the door-step.

Thus dismissed, Phyllis went forth. With a sad heart, she walked along a bleak, bare road, feeling every blast of the cold northern wind through her thin camlet gown; but she was warm enough by the time she reached the farm-house. It was shut up—all the people were gone to a neighbouring fair; only an angry dog, who growled at her from behind the door, had been left within. Phyllis wandered about disconsolately till she came to a little wood already turning sere and red beneath the grey wintry sky. Footsore and weary, the child took the first path she found. Scarcely had she walked a few steps when she saw an old brown rock covered with green mosses and patches of hoary lichens, and beneath it there bubbled forth a clear spring, which widened into a broad pool covered with a very forest of watercresses. This then, was the goal of her journey. Phyllis was very tired, and the first thing she did was to sit down by the rock and rest. The spot was green and lonely, yet the child was not afraid. Maybe she felt all unconsciously that unkind voice and unkind eyes could not reach her here, and so she let the sweetness and tender calm of nature fall on her little troubled heart. Never, it seemed to Phyllis, had she seen anything so pretty and so green as this spot. Summer still lingered here, if not in its warmth, at least in its lovely verdure. A tuft of hart's tongue grew under the rock, and the long green glossy leaves drooped above the water. Delicate grasses and tall reeds waved in every little breath of wind, and pale blue flowers blossomed on the sandy bank, against which the rippling water broke at the poor, tired feet of little Phyllis.

At length she was rested, and set about her task. It was harder of accomplishment than Phyllis had imagined it to be. The watercresses grew in the middle of the pool, and every time she tried to reach them she slipped down the edge of the bank into the water. She was soon wet up to the knees, and still the watercresses remained far away, inaccessible, and grew like a fairy isle. Phyllis tried them from every side of the pool; she bent over the rock to reach at them, and nearly tumbled into the water, and still those provoking cresses kept in their stronghold, and thence seemed to bid defiance to all her efforts. The water was so shallow, and Phyllis was so wet, that she might as well have waded through to get her booty; but that little dark pool on whose heart the gloomy shadow of the trees was lying seemed unfathomably deep to the timid child, so she stood on the edge, hopeless of accomplishing the task that had been laid upon her; and, fearful of returning home without having accomplished it, she wrung her hands in her helplessness and distress, and, at length, fairly giving way, she sat down and burst into tears.

Many and bitter were the thoughts that came to Phyllis as she wept. She knew that her father was noble and rich; why then was she the drudge and the servant of these strange women? This very spot might belong to the Marquis, for all his little daughter could say to the contrary, for he owned many a broad acre of the land that lay about his château. Was it not then a hard fate, that she, his child, should be sitting thus on the bare earth, her wet clothes clinging to her shivering limbs, and her heart sinking within her at the thought of going back empty-handed to the stern task-mistress who had been set over her? Yes, it was a hard lot, and the more Phyllis thought over it, the more she wept and gave way to her sorrow. And now it happened to her as it so often happens in the fairy tales: when the clouds are heaviest some bright sun-

beam comes and pierces them. Little
Phyllis was sitting thus, feeling all forlorn and quite heart-broken, when help
came to her.

Tramp, tramp, sounded a horse's hoofs
along the road—for the pool was on the
skirt of the wood—and as the tramp grew
nearer there came with it a rushing sound
through the thicket, and a dog ran down
to the water's edge and began drinking
eagerly by her side. Phyllis ceased her
weeping to look at him. He was the most
beautiful dog she had ever seen—silky,
brown with white paws, a white star on
his forehead, and a brass collar, bright
as gold, round his neck. When the dog
had done drinking he went sniffing round
Phyllis, who remained quiet, for she was
afraid; then he sat down by her and
looked at her with his big brown eyes,
so clear and so honest, whilst his red
tongue lolled out of his mouth. It seemed
to Phyllis as if he were trying to understand her trouble, and were asking her,
in his canine way, to tell him all about it.

She shook her head at him with a sigh, and stretching out her little hand, stroked his brown coat, softly saying, like a child as she was: ".It is no use telling you, for you know you could not help me."

As she thus addressed him, she bent to see what name was inscribed on the dog's collar, and with a start and a flush of surprise, she read:

F I D è L E
Belongs to the Count of Saint Brice.

This dog's master was the young Count whom, for his mother's sake, her step-mother so hated; that Corydon whom she had not seen for seven years, but whom she remembered so well. Meanwhile, the tramp, tramp of the horse's hoofs was now close by. A shrill whistle called the truant away, and as he did not obey the summons, a clear young voice called out, "Fidèle."

But Fidèle only whined and barked, perplexed. For some reason or other he would not leave Phyllis. His master, who knew that all this land belonged to

the Marquis de la Faille, and who feared
lest the dog should run down the game of
a gentleman between whom and himself
there was little love, alighted hastily and
went to seek him.

Burning with shame at her humbled
and fallen state, Phyllis crept round the
rock and hid herself as the young man
came up calling the dog. But he saw her,
and said kindly, " Do not hide, child: I
will not hurt you !" Phyllis, however, did
not stir, so the Count, who had some
natural curiosity in him, walked round
the rock and found her standing there,
with her back towards him and her face
hidden in her hands.

" I tell you, child, I will not hurt you,"
he said again, and gently compelling her
to turn round, he removed her hands from
her crimson face.

Bitter was Phyllis's shame at appearing
thus, in her coarse grey camlet gown,
so wet and unseemly, before the young
Corydon who had once seen her in all the
splendour of a white silk petticoat and red

velvet bodice. She felt as if she must have sunk down to the very earth and been swallowed up by it, when, looking up at him, now grown to man's estate, she saw him so handsome, so gay, in a hunting-suit of grey laid with gold. She only hoped he would not know her again. Vain hope! The young Count's olive cheek grew flushed, his bright dark eyes lit. "Phyllis," he cried, "why you are my Phyllis!"

But on that first cry of surprise and joy followed the saddest wonder. "Phyllis, what brings you here alone? And you are all wet and shivering! Why, my little Phyllis, what has happened?"

She gazed up in his face. She read the tender kindness there, kindness all for her, so long unused to the sweet food; and being but a child, she threw her arms around him and cried piteously. When Phyllis was calmer, she found herself sitting again on the grassy earth; the young Count was sitting by her side, chafing her cold hands in his, and Fidèle

—to keep her warm, no doubt—had coiled himself at her feet. Phyllis related her little sad story to her old friend. He made no comments, but heard her with mingled wrath and sorrow. Fame had already told him strange tales of Madame du Mésnil's two beautiful daughters; Phyllis was still very young—a mere child; but these ladies should not be her companions. He resolved that they should not tempt her to folly and sin if he could prevent it. Of all this, however, he said not a word. His silence awed Phyllis, and feeling somewhat shy, she made a timid attempt to rise.

"I must try again and get the watercresses," she said, with a sigh. "I dare not go home without them."

"I shall get you plenty," he said, kindly; "do not think of that, or of those women, Phyllis. Be guided by me, and all will go well with you. Tell no one that we have met—not a soul."

"Oh! no, no," answered Phyllis, shaking her little wise head, as much as to say that she knew better.

"I do not know when we shall meet again," he resumed.

"I can come for more watercresses to-morrow," suggested Phyllis, in her inno-cence.

"I shall be far away by to-morrow," said the young Count, smiling, "and who knows, Phyllis, if you and I shall ever meet again?"

She heard him with a blank face. He had come down from heaven itself to com-fort her, it seemed, and now he was going away; going perhaps for ever!

"But I will not leave France," con-tinued the Count, "without seeing you righted, Phyllis. I will go to the King himself in Versailles, and tell him how you, his poor little subject, are treated. Those cruel women shall not hold you in bondage a week longer, Phyllis, not one."

But Phyllis did not heed these promises of future good. She looked up in his face till her eyes were blinded with tears.

"And shall I not see you again?" she

asked, clinging to him; "never, never again?"

The young Count hesitated. He was bound on a daring and dangerous task. The breezes which now blew over France spoke but faintly of shepherds and their lambs, but told in a clarion voice, loud and shrill, of freedom and equality and the rights of man; and the young Count, once so haughty, having caught the fever of the times, was going to join the Marquis de la Fayette, and to fight with him for American liberty. He might come back, indeed, from the war; but he might also leave his young bones in that strange land and never more see the face of Phyllis.

"Nay; I may come back," he said, hopefully. "I may come back, Phyllis."

"Then, promise that you will," she cried, almost impetuously; "for if you promise, I know you will do it."

The pathetic faith of this poor forlorn child went to the young Count's heart. He did not promise, but he looked down in her face with tender pity. This little

Phyllis, whom he remembered bright as a rose, was now pale as a lily. Her eyes were sad, her lips were wan, her young beauty had vanished; only her golden hair was unchanged, also that little black mole which nestled near her dimpled chin. It was by that mole he had known her again, and now, as he looked at it, his heart began to beat. Then all at once the dream of his boyhood came back to him, and it returned with the fervour of his young manhood.

"Phyllis," he said, with some vehémence, "I do promise to come back to you, "but you must also keep the promise you made seven years ago. Will you?"

Phyllis too remembered the old compact, for her little face became very red, but she said, " Yes," at once.

The Count drew a gold ring from his little finger, and put it upon the biggest finger he could find in her childish hand, but it was still too large, and would fit none.

" I shall wear it round my neck," said Phyllis joyfully; " I know they would take it from me."

"Until you give me back that ring—my mother's wedding-ring," said the Count, "I am yours; and until I ask it again you are mine. Is it so?"

"Yes," said Phyllis, turning pale with the solemnity of the pledge; " it is so."

"And now we must part; good-bye, my Phyllis; good-bye, my dear wife."

They rose. The Count took this child-wife of his in his arms and kissed the black mole on her cheek with tender devotion. No knight ever loved his lady, no young bridegroom ever loved his young bride, more fondly than the young Count loved this little, pale, sorrowful Phyllis then.

" Good-bye," she sobbed : " good-bye, but oh! do come back soon; and oh! please will you get me some watercresses before you go?"

" Ay, that I will," said Corydon, setting his teeth; " but let them dare to use you so much longer, my Phyllis; let them !"

When he had gathered watercresses enough, he said again that it was time to go, and again they parted. Phyllis kissed her lover and kissed Fidèle; then the young man rode away, and his dog followed him, not without casting a wistful look behind; and Phyllis, sitting down once more on the edge of the pool, felt very sorrowful and very happy; for if her fairy prince was gone, "He will come back," thought Phyllis; "he will come back."

The young Count too had his thoughts as he rode away. Little childish Phyllis, the watercresses, and his mother's ring were all running in his head. He felt rather astonished to find himself solemnly pledged to a child with a black mole. What if the black mole were at the bottom of it all! Magic was not quite over yet in those days, and witches all had moles. Was this little Phyllis a witch? "She may be what she likes," thought the young soldier of La Fayette, with a great throb of love at his heart. "Never shall I wed another woman than this one— never, never."

In the meanwhile Phyllis went home

with her watercresses, and caught a bad cold for having been wet, and a severe scolding for having remained out so long. And the young Count who left Saint Brice that same night, saw the King in Versailles, and told him her story. So before the week was out, before even the Count sailed across the Atlantic, His Majesty sent down a special messenger to remove Mlle. de la Faille from the house of Madame du Mésnil and place her in a convent, to be educated there with other noble damsels, until her father should take her once more under his own care.

Five years had gone by. The Marquis de la Faille was sitting in his chair, wrapped in a long, quilted morning-gown ; a white night-cap came down to his very eyebrows, and the gay Némorin twirled his thumbs and stared at a fly buzzing against the window-panes in the autumn sun.

"My love," he plaintively said to his wife, who sat near him at her tambour-frame, "do tell that fly not to buzz so."

Madame did not answer, but gave him, and everything around her a moody look. The room was a splendid room, no one could deny it. The gardens below were green and lovely; the fountains were playing gaily, and the dancing fawns and nymphs looked white and merry in the sunshine. But what availed splendid home, green garden, and money, if Madame de la Faille could not enjoy them?

The man she had married was an idiot for life, and she was tied to his sickness: an unwilling nurse. Pleasure was denied her; although his death would give her liberty, it could not give her wealth as well. The Marquis had made no will, and the girl whom her step-mother kept mewed up in a room of the château would inherit all her father's property. Madame de la Faille had made a bad bargain.

The Marchioness was brooding over the whole story, and not heeding poor old Némorin's querulous request that she would tell the fly not to buzz, when a servant came up with a message. The

Count of Saint Brice was below, and asked
to see the Marquis. So he had returned
from America, where he had been fighting
under La Fayette. What was he like?
she wondered, and what errand made him
seek her husband? Perplexed and curious,
she bade the Count be shown up. When
he entered the room, in a suit of silver
and grey, the lady thought she had never
seen a young man of aspect so noble and
prepossessing as the son of her betrayed
friend. She gazed at him graciously, and
seeing the involuntary start of surprise he
gave on looking at the Marquis, she heaved
a deep, tender sigh, bade him welcome, and
said to her husband :

"My love, the Count of Saint Brice has
come to see you."

"Let him tell the fly not to buzz so,"
answered poor Némorin.

The Marchioness took out her handkerchief and stifled a sob, whilst her visitor
gazed with sorrow and surprise on the
ruin before him.

"Madame," said the Count, addressing

the lady, after a pause, " I perceive your unfortunate husband cannot attend to me : in your hands, therefore, lies my fate. Through you, I ask Monsieur de la Faille for the hand of his daughter."

On hearing this, all signs of favour vanished from the lady's face, and she coldly answered :

" You are very good, sir : but my husband has no wish to see his daughter married just yet."

" Madame," replied the Count, " this refusal comes not from him, but from you."

Madame de la Faille did not attempt to deny this. Resting her arm across the tambour-frame, she looked moodily at her guest. Then, after a long pause, she said, with a dark smile :

" Pray, when did you last see my step-daughter ?"

" Five years ago."

" But you have had some glimpse of her since your return."

" Madame, I arrived last night."

" And you ask her in marriage this morning, though you have not seen her for five years ?"

" Madame, I do."

" Well, sir, for the sake of constancy so rare, also because your mother and I were friends once, I shall grant your request; but, like the wicked fairy in the story, I lay down three conditions. Do you agree, first, to marry Mademoiselle de la Faille without a dowry ?"

" I do, and gladly."

" Secondly, my beloved husband's health not allowing him to be disturbed in any fashion, and on any account, are you satisfied that the marriage shall take place in the chapel of your castle ?"

" Madame, I am satisfied."

" Thirdly, as, on account of my dear husband's illness, I can allow no courtship or wooing, are you content not to see your bride till you meet her on the morning of your wedding-day ?"

The young Count gave a start.

" Madame, that is impossible."

" Then, sir, I cannot grant your suit."

He tried to move her, but she was in-
exorable.

" Madame," he said, warmly, " no
change which may have taken place in
Mademoiselle de la Faille's appearance
can alter my feelings ; but in honour I
must ascertain what hers are before I
marry her."

The lady brooded awhile, and her face
was not pleasant to look at when she was
thus meditating ; then she coldly informed
the Count that she would allow him to
see her step-daughter once, namely, on
the eve of his wedding-day, which she left
him free to fix. He tried hard to get
better terms, but failed. He yielded, but,
indignant at her harshness, he emphatically assured her that if he detected the
least signs of reluctance in Mademoiselle
de la Faille, he should set her free, no
matter at what risk.

" Sir, you are wrong to mistrust your
own powers of fascination," was her ironical reply. " Mademoiselle de la Faille will

never reject so accomplished a gentleman, and so rare a lover."

On this they parted—the lady triumphant at having prevailed, the Count angry at being conquered; and—why deny it?—rather troubled at terms which were harsh even for an age in which, 'spite its arcadian fancies, the feelings of noble damsels were very rarely consulted.

"Oh, my Phyllis!" he could not help saying to himself, as he rode home. "What has happened to you, my darling? What cruel disease or fatal accident has come to wither your youth?—for beauty you had not. You have shed bitter tears since we parted near this very spot, my Phyllis; but now, please Heaven, your troubles and sorrows are over, and faithful love is yours for ever." Chivalry is undying, though the age of chivalry has gone by, and chivalry was strong in the young Count's heart. It blended with and tempered all his feelings, and though now put to so severe a test, it was not found wanting. When disquieting thoughts would come, suggesting that Phyllis had had the small-pox, or lost an eye, or undergone some terrible change for the worse, this faithful lover bade them avaunt, and only hurried on the preparations for his marriage. At length the rooms which were being fitted up, prepared at much cost for the young Countess, were ready, the day was fixed, and, on the eve of that eventful day, the Count rode forth to see his Phyllis, and learn his fate. But he did not think of that. All his apprehensions, all his fears, were gone, and a great sense of happiness had come in their stead. The day was a beautiful autumn day, full of a mellow, golden light. As the Count rode through the little wood, near the pool of watercresses, it seemed to him that the birds warbled love-songs on every bough, and that the soft breeze which passed through the trees was laden with fragrance as delicious as any breeze that ever blew in fairyland. For were not the great thoughts of his boyhood, and the great desire of his youth, going to be fulfilled at last? Was he not going to wed his Phyllis on the morrow?

But when the Count reached the château of La Faille, when he went up the steps and crossed the threshold, there is no denying that his mood was much subdued. All the doubts and fears which he had kept at bay came back to him with cruel power. He dreaded this much-wished-for meeting; especially did he fear lest his countenance should betray a painful surprise, which might wound his Phyllis's tender heart. Devoutly did he pray that however she might be altered, and whatever he might feel, she might read nothing in his eyes save the strong love which had never ceased, and never should cease, he trusted, to burn in his heart for her. That heart throbbed rather fast as he entered the room in which the Marquis and his wife were sitting. A young girl stood in the furthest window, but her face was turned from him, and she neither moved nor looked round on his entrance.

"Well, sir," said the Marquise, in a

mocking tone, "you are a punctual man, and I keep my word of course. My love, this is the Count of Saint Brice, whom you are to marry to-morrow morning. Will you not look at us?"

But instead of obeying, the young girl only buried her face in her hands, and all the poor, puzzled young Count could see was a slender, graceful figure, standing very still in the sunshine which poured in through the tall window.

" Well, sir," resumed the elder lady, in the same mocking tone, " you shall not think or say that I lay any constraint on this coy bride of yours. I leave her with her father and you."

She rose and left the room as she spoke. So long as the train of her silk dress swept the polished floor, so long as her stately figure had not vanished behind the panelled door, the Count did not stir. His heart indeed fluttered wildly in his breast, but his olive cheek, and his bright dark eye, betrayed no emotion. When the room, however, was empty of Madame de la Faille's presence, when he was fairly alone with his love and her poor, old, foolish father, who leaned back in his chair, twirling his thumb, as usual, all self-control left him.

" Phyllis, my Phyllis," he cried, " have we met at last—at last !" and in a second he was by her side, gently, but vainly, endeavouring to remove her hands.

" My Phyllis," he pleaded, " what do you fear ? Not that I should love you less : that is impossible; not that I should take advantage of the bondage in which you live: that, too, is impossible. Then look at me, remember our old love; look at me—above all, trust in me."

His voice faltered a little as he said the words, for something terrible, he thought, must be hidden behind those little white hands which still resisted his. At length they yielded, revealing a face so witching, and so beautiful, that, through very wonder, the Count let them drop, and started back. Thus they stood for a moment in the old window, he amazed and doubtful, she blushing like a rose in the warm sun-light.

"Forgive me," he said, recovering, with a deep sigh, "but you are so altered that I cannot yet conquer my amazement. Are you really, can you be, my Phyllis?"

Again his eager gaze scanned her lovely face. The charming profile, and the pretty Grecian lip of his Phyllis, he knew, but white powder hid the bright hair, another soul seemed to look through the blue eyes, the smile of the rosy lips had another meaning. The Count's dainty, delicate lily-of-the-valley had turned into a garden rose, gorgeous and beautiful in the bloom of its eighteen summers. The change was so great that involuntarily he looked for the mole which he had kissed on the day of their parting; it was still there, near her white, dimpled chin.

"Well," she asked, laughing softly at his perplexed looks, "am I Phyllis?"

"Forgive me," he said again; "but how could I expect to find you grown so very, very beautiful?"

E 2

She smiled at his praise, but smiled like one who knew that praise her due. That bright, fond smile dazzled him.

"Ah!" he said, with involuntary transport, "how could your step-mother be so cruel? I thought some terrible disease had disfigured you, and I find you so lovely, so lovely!" he repeated, taking her hand, and looking in her witching face.

"And you would have married me all the same?"

"Can you ask it?"

"And loved me all the same?"

"Ah! Phyllis, Phyllis, can you doubt it?"

"I have learned to doubt many things," she replied, with some bitterness.

"Because you have been unhappy, my Phyllis?"

She threw up her arms almost wildly. Unhappy! she had been wretched, utterly wretched since they had parted. And suddenly laying her head on his shoulder, she began to weep. He did his best to comfort her, but the task was not an easy one. " Would he love her—was he sure he would love her—would he never repent having married her?" she asked, with sobs and tears, almost impetuously, and scarcely giving him time to answer. If her distress had not been so great, the Count would have felt provoked at these questions. And yet, strange to say, there was something in his heart, something deep and far away, which almost justified them. On seeing this girl's blooming face, his first feelings had been amazement, as if he were gazing on a stranger; then joy, the natural delight of a young man at finding a handsome bride instead of a plain one, had followed; but his third and last feeling, which deepened as it went on, had been one of dull, heavy disappointment. This Phyllis was very lovely, but then she no longer seemed the same pale little Phyllis whom he had dreamed of for five years, and that one it was whom he had loved, remembered, and come back to wed: forgetting that the child had become a woman. He looked at the beautiful face which lay so near his, and wondered that he felt so cold. With an impulse which he knew later to have been a last despairing effort to save his drowning love, he suddenly stooped to press his lips on that little mole which had once worked such wonders. But either its magic was gone, or the perverse fate which delights in thwarting lovers had resolved to vex the Count, for Phyllis, on seeing his intentions, drew back with a sudden cry, whilst a voice behind them said, angrily :

" Go to your room at once, Mademoiselle. As for you, sir, you may put off that kiss till to-morrow."

Poor Phyllis turned to the nearest door, and vanished in a twinkling; whilst the Count, blushing like a girl, stammered an apology. The Marquise would hear of none : she was a lady of the strictest decorum, but scolded him so sharply that the poor Marquis began to weep, and the Count was glad to be gone.

And glad surely Philip de Saint Brice ought to have been as he rode home. But, alas for the frailty of the human heart! the golden glory of the day had fled, the songs of birds were as dirges for the fading year, and the breeze no longer blew from fairyland, but came laden with the chill breath of winter. The cruel ordeal was over; Phyllis was far more beautiful than his fondest dreams had ever pictured her to be; she was to be his on the morrow, and the Count felt the most miserable of men. Alas! for the rash vows of youth. Alas! for his rash faith in the truth of his own heart— he no longer loved her. He tried to doubt it, but could not. He had loved a dream all these years. And now that he had reached the fulness of his desires, now that he had stood on the eve of their accomplishment, they were cold and dead.

" This is the last day of my liberty," he thought, as he reached his home, and went up the winding turret staircase.

" I must not repine, I must not complain: I have willed it so. The man must abide by the boy's folly. Oh! Phyllis, my little Phyllis, whom I carried up these very stairs eleven years ago, you shall never know what a change these years have wrought in your boyish lover's heart. You shall never be made to feel that what you had then is gone for ever for us both. You have lost the love, and I, the greater bankrupt of the two, my Phyllis, I have lost the power of loving. You are bright and beautiful as the day, but never again can I love you as when I acted Corydon with you; never again can I feel as I felt when I met you, and, taking you in my arms, a poor, pale child, whose cheeks were sunk with grief, and whose eyes were red with weeping, vowed that you, and you alone, should be my wife."

The Count sighed as the word wife recalled him from these fond dreams of the past to the reality of the morrow. He had reached the upper room in which Phyllis and he had spent an hour once.

He looked again on a vast sea; he saw a stormy sky. He thought of his blooming bride, who would soon survey that sea and sky with him, standing by his side with her hand clasped in his, her head resting tenderly on his shoulder; and he tried to feel a lover's transports. He tried, but could not; love was dead in his heart, dead and buried, and even beauty could not waken it back to life, or give it a second birth. So the Count de Saint Brice set his teeth and knit his brows.

" Love is dead," he thought, " but honour does not die. Honour must and shall do instead of love."

The sun was going down, throned in purple clouds. The Count watched its setting till it had vanished in the deep, dark sea, above which a ruddy light lingered awhile, but awhile only. The night was moonless and starless. Huge clouds spreading from the south-west soon covered the whole sky; a stormy wind rose, and moaned along the shore; and the tide came up the beach, filling the dark night with its loud, angry roaring.

"My Phyllis will have but a stormy welcome to-morrow," sighed the Count, as he turned from the window and called for a light. "Well, poor Phyllis, this a a rude home for her; but maybe she will find a way to make it pleasant."

"I shall spend the night here," he said to the old servant, who brought him a lamp. "Let me have some supper, and a bottle of the old Burgundy."

Gertrude stared; there was no bed in the room : nothing, save an old arm-chair; but already the Count's servants had learned that to hear and to obey was their lot; so she withdrew without uttering a word. She soon came back with a cold pasty, and a square bottle of Burgundy, covered with the dust and cobwebs of half a century. The Count looked at it moodily. "That wine was bottled when my grandfather married my grandmother, after she had had the small-pox," he thought, with a sigh. "She offered to set him free, but he was a proud man, and he would marry her all the same, only he never loved her again, and it is said the poor lady did well to die when my father was born. Yours shall never be so hard a lot, my Phyllis, never." And pouring himself out a glass of the rich, red wine, the Count drank to the happiness of his bride, even though his own should be the cost. When his glass was empty he filled it again; when his bottle was drained he called for another; and the pasty, with its crust like brown gold, and its rich savoury viands, remained untouched. Trouble was with the Count of Saint Brice on the eve of his wedding-day. He was not hungry, and even the generous vintage which had ripened on Burgundian hills could not deaden, or make him forget his strange desolation. A torpor did, indeed, come over him; he sat by the table, his elbows resting on it, his cheeks in the palms of his hands, his eyes staring moodily at his empty glass; and he knew that he had a grief, though what that

grief was he no longer remembered.   Thus
he remained, till he sank back in his chair
and slept a long, dreamless sleep, during
which he was conscious of a moaning
wind, and of rain beating against the
window-panes.

" I told her to wait below, but she would
come up.   A little forward thing !" said a
querulous voice in his ear.

The young Count woke up with a start.
Gertrude stood before him with a sour
look on her face, and by her side stood a
slender girl, whose garments were heavy
with rain.

Whilst the Count brooded over his
troubles, Gertrude and the other servants
were gathered round the kitchen-fire,
listening to the wind and rain, and to the
moaning of the sea.   They speculated on
the next day's weather, and on their
future mistress's temper.   Would the sun
shine a bright welcome on the bride, and
would the young Countess be a pretty
butterfly like the last, all for pastorals
and   idylls,   and   wisely   allowing   her

servants to have their own way; or would she be like her predecessor, the poor lady who had had the small-pox, and whose sharp tongue and shrill voice were still remembered by Gertrude?

" There were no cards and no plays in those days, I can tell you," said Gertrude, nodding severely at two idle damsels who were playing at pigeon-vole in the corner. " It was all spinning and cooking and sewing."

Here the kitchen-door was gently pushed open; a young, pale girl, in a long cloak and a little black hat, stepped in, then stood still in the bright, ruddy glow of the kitchen-fire.

" Please," she said softly, " I want to speak to the Count of Saint Brice."

They all stared at her in amazement, which, with Gertrude, would have turned into downright anger, if she had not remembered that the seamstress from the town was to send one of her workwomen to sew on the lace for the young bride's quilt. So, whilst the two girls in the corner left off their pigeon-vole to look open-mouthed at this girl, so pale, so fair, and with unpowdered hair, which clustered like rings of gold around her graceful neck, Gertrude lit a candle, and with a sharp, " Come this way," showed the stranger upstairs. She took her to the rooms which had once belonged to the Count's mother, and which he had fitted up at heavy expense, and in much haste, for his bride. The silken hangings, splendid mirrors, and rich carpets looked very gorgeous even by the dull, flickering light which Gertrude held.

" Well," she said, standing still by a lofty bed all blue and silvery, " make haste now, and sew on the lace. I shall hold the light for you. But a pretty thing your mistress did to wait till this time of the night to finish the quilt, and the Count getting married to-morrow."

The stranger started back.

" I bring no lace," she said. " I come to speak to the Count on pressing business."

Gertrude stared, then tossed up her

head. And what pressing business, she should like to know, could a girl of her years have with the Count on the eve of his wedding-day?

"It is because this is the eve of the Count's wedding-day that I have business with him," composedly replied the stranger. "Make haste; this is a pressing matter, I tell you, and I have a long way before me."

"I knew the girls would be all after my master," muttered Gertrude; but she dare not keep back the Count's visitor; so she went up the turret-stairs, followed, 'spite her protests, by the stranger, and thus it was that they both came into the Count's presence. He rose, surprised and doubtful. The young girl turned to Gertrude.

"Leave us," she said, quietly; "my business with your master is private."

"Business, indeed! Pretty business to come stealing up after me, when I told you to wait below!"

"Leave us," interrupted the Count; and this time the order was obeyed, though not without some grumbling about forward demoiselles and the time of the night. The stranger quietly shut the door after Gertrude, then taking up the lamp from the table, and holding it so that its light fell full on her face, she said calmly:

"Do you know me?"

Oh, heavens! did he know her?—did he know the lost love of his boyhood?—did he know the radiant eyes that had looked up at him so tenderly, when, taking her in his arms, a poor, pale child, he had vowed to love and cherish her as his own dear wife? Five years had given her the charm and the bloom of maiden youth, but there she stood before him, with the light of the lamp shining on her sweet, fair face and on her clustering golden hair, his darling Phyllis still. He could not move, he could not speak, he could scarcely breathe; he could only look at her with silent, delighted eyes.

"You know me," she said, putting down the lamp. "Few words will do. That past which you have set aside was very dear to me. It has brought me here through wind and rain, and at heavy risk, to save you from a great sin. Whilst I have your promise and your mother's wedding ring, how can you marry another woman? From the one I release you, and the other I restore. Here it is; take it, and give it to your wife to-morrow, if it so please you. You are free now, and there is not a creature breathing, not one, who can say there is a stain on your honour."

She put the ring on the table and looked at him sadly and proudly, with dim eyes and a pale, quivering lip. But he did not take up the pledge she thus relinquished: he had neither heard nor heeded her words. The first amazement of his joy had gone by, and, taking her in his arms, he gave way to the rapture of his heart.

" Oh, my love, my dear heart !" he cried, in the language of the day, " have I got you back? Were you lost, and have I got you back, never more to let you go—never, never," said he, kissing the golden hair on which rain-drops still shone. Then he gently put her a little away from him, but only the better to look down into her silent, wondering face.

"Phyllis," he said, eagerly, "to-morrow was to have been the darkest day in my life, but you have come to make it the brightest. Now that you have entered this house, you must never leave it again, unless as its mistress. It is ready for you, Phyllis, ready and waiting. And listen, that is thunder; look, that is lightning!" he added, as a broad, bright flash filled the room. "Providence sent you, and Providence will not let you leave me again. How can you doubt? What need you fear? Have we not been pledged years, and has not your father consented to my marriage with his daughter? Oh, my Phyllis, say yes, and let us not run the risk of being again separated."

He ceased, and rousing herself from her long amazement, she untwined his arms from around her, left his side, then suddenly coming back to him, she put her two hands on his shoulders and looked deep into his eyes, with a searching glance.

"Philip," she said, "whom were you going to marry to morrow? For whom did you get those rooms prepared which I have just seen below?"

"For my Phyllis," he replied, smiling fondly. "I got that cage ready for my darling bird who now stands there, shy and mistrustful, before me, who looks, and will not come in."

So he had been true all the time. So, unless by taking the name of his little pale Phyllis, Manon's brilliant beauty could not have lured him. So he had been true, though so nearly cheated out of his love and liberty by that false Florimel. She did not change her attitude or remove her look. Still standing with her two hands resting lightly on his shoulders, and her eyes raised to his, she said, sadly, but, though she did not mean it, very tenderly:

"Do you know what you are doing? Do you know that if you marry me you take me as I am, with these clothes for my only dowry? Do you know that my poor father no longer knows his child, and that I was a prisoner in his house, and that I could not have escaped to-night if my step-mother had not been too much engaged with the nuptials of her niece to-morrow, to watch me? Do you know that if you cast off Manon du Mésnil for me, you make two keen and bitter enemies, and must prepare for long, maybe for life-long trouble?"

He looked down, smiling, with grave fondness, in her face, and he answered: "Do you know that the first moment I saw you, when we were both children, I loved you? Do you know that when I met you five years ago, when you were still but a child in looks and in years, I felt, 'This girl I will marry and none other?' Do you know that if I had found you as sickly, as pale, and as unlovely as I left you, instead of being the beautiful and blooming girl now before me, I should have loved you still as I love you now: infinitely, my Phyllis, and for ever, with a love which neither sickness nor sorrow nor death itself shall ever remove from my heart ?"

He ceased, unable to say more ; and she remained silent, unable to answer. He who spoke believed every word he uttered, and she who listened believed it no less. Do not wonder then that he prevailed, and do not think poor lonely Phyllis indiscreet, if, having come through the rain and storm to save her lover's honour, she remained in the fond, warm shelter of his faithful home and heart, rather than venture out again in the bleak, wild night, and return to the house which had become her prison.

How the marriage ceremony went off in the chapel of the old feudal castle, there is no record to tell ; but it is asserted that the suddenness of the whole affair nearly sent Gertrude into a fit, and that on her recovery she was heard to exclaim : " I knew the girls would all be running after our young master when he came back so handsome, but I never expected anything like *that*."

At ten of the morning the Count was to fetch his bride, but by eight he stood at the gates of the château—two hours' impatience is no doubt natural in a bridegroom—and asked to see its mistress. Madame de la Faille had quarrelled that very morning with her waiting-maid, who seized this opportunity for a sly bit of revenge. So she took the Count upstairs at once, and perfidiously throwing a door open, she showed him in, without warning, to the dressing-room where her mistress, with brush in hand, was endeavouring to put a mole on the cheek of the beautiful Manon. The two ladies started back apart on seeing him, and Madame de la Faille, running up to the Count, put her two hands on his shoulders and tried to push him out, saying, playfully, "Not yet, sir, not yet: you come too soon;" but the Count did not stir, and looking sorrowfully at the young lady, who had turned her blushing face away, he said, gravely :

"I do not come too early for my purpose, Madame, which is to tell you that I was married to your step-daughter, Mademoiselle de la Faille, last night."

The Marquise remained thunder-struck, but the young lady uttered a faint cry, and sank down on a chair, like one overcome with shame and grief. The Marquise set her teeth and clenched her hands, giving her blue taffetas morning-wrapper a dab of black paint from the brush which she still held.

"Well, sir," she said, "is that what your boasted honour and constancy come to? Was it all meant to insult my daughter; or have you really been deceived by some artful impostor; and do you come here, unconscious of the cheat that has been practised upon you?"

"Attempted," corrected the Count. And locking sadly at Manon, who was weeping, he said, gently: "Allow me to regret that gifts so precious and so rare as youth and perfect beauty should be thus wasted."

Mademoiselle du Mésnil wept more than

ever, but her aunt, seizing the Count by the arm, said, imperiously: "Come to my husband, sir; come and account for this insult to his daughter."

"Madame," said the Count, coldly, "not to your husband only, but to the whole world, will I answer for what I have done."

"Come to my husband, sir," repeated the lady, exasperated at his coolness. She pushed a door open, and they stood together in a stately bed-room. It was darkened, yet the Count could see the poor Marquis sitting in his bed, propped up by pillows, with the flush from the crimson curtains on his pallid face.

"Marquis!" said the enraged lady, "this is the Count of Saint Brice, the son of the foolish little Countess who used to act so badly, you know. Well, then, this is her son, Marquis, who has been stealing your daughter from you, do you hear? He has lured her to his house, and disgraced you and her. Do you hear, I say, do you hear?"

She took his arm and shook it, in the violence of her wrath. Her fury woke the palsied man back to life.

" Is it fire?" he gasped, " is it for murder?" He tried to rise, but could not, and, with a wild look of horror and a convulsive groan, he sank back—dead!

The Marquise screamed, the Count called for help ; but when help came it availed not. The shock had proved mortal to the poor, enfeebled body.

" You have killed him!" cried the Marquise, when she realized that she was a widow. " Leave the house, sir,"

" Madame," gravely replied the Count, " this house belongs now to my dear wife, the Marquis's daughter, and I shall stay here to guard her rights till she can come herself and make them good."

The Marquise, on hearing this, raved like one demented. Decency and respect for that poor dead man, who lay cold and white beneath his crimson daïs, had no power to restrain her. The Count was shocked, and to avoid the unseemly quar-

rel, he left the room. But he still remained in the château, whence he des-
patched a messenger with a letter for his
Phyllis, whom he bade come to him at
once. We cannot quarrel with the dead :
all our wrath spends itself in vain upon
them : they lie beyond our reach, in their
solemn silence. The Marquise grew
hushed at once, when the Count left her ;
she, too, soon forsook her dead husband,
and went to seek her niece. The servants heard the two ladies talking loud
and angrily for some time, then they grew
suddenly silent, and a great hush, the
hush of death, fell over the whole of the
stately mansion.

The Count sat alone in the large salon,
feeling the cloud which death had cast
over his new-born happiness, and waiting
for his Phyllis. But time passed : it was
noon now, and Phyllis came not. The
Count paced the salon up and down, in a
fever of unrest, at the bottom of which
lurked secret fears—those shadows which
darken our sunniest hours, and throw

their gloom upon the brightness of our
lives. At length, when another hour had
gone by, he could bear the suspense no
longer. He went down to the stable,
took out his horse himself, and rode off,
without saying a word to anyone.

The Count remained two hours away;
when he came galloping back to the gates
of the château, he was pale as death, and
his panting horse was covered with foam.

"My wife!—where is my wife?" he
cried. "Phyllis, Phyllis!" But no Phyllis
answered him; not a soul appeared at his
call. He alighted, he hastened up the
broad staircase, he went through the
rooms, and he saw no one. The whole
of that great house was deserted. Death
had entered it, he had set up his grim
throne there, and now reigned alone.

Everyone had fled: the Marquise with
the plate and the family jewels; the upper
servants with such plunder as they could
lay their hands on. The dead-chamber
alone had not been ransacked; there the
Marquis slept his last sleep, with his old

dog, who had crept up to him and was now lying at his feet. Like one distracted, the Count went through the whole house, seeking his Phyllis. Once his heart throbbed with joy as he heard a step, but when he pushed open a door, he only saw an old woman, who shook her head at all his questions, and said, in a quavering voice : " Deaf, sir, deaf : stone deaf," and, putting a slip of paper in his hand, went away muttering.

Mechanically the Count looked at the paper, and read :

" Because for half an hour you have loved me with the only true love that ever has been, or ever will be, felt for the un-happy Manon, I will serve you. Watch over your love, and beware of ' Thetis.' "

" Beware of ' Thetis !' " thought the amazed Count. Then suddenly he uttered a cry, " Oh Heaven !"

The ' Thetis' was one of the King's ships in the harbour. It might be ordered for Pondichéry; it might be going away the next day, that very night—it might be gone by this. The Count was a brave man, but no coward's cheek ever grew whiter with fear than his, as he stood with the fatal paper in his hand. There are evils too strong for the strongest man, and this was one. The Count knew that he could avenge his wife—he did not know if he could save her. He could hunt her ravishers to the very confines of the earth, and wring their heart's blood from them; he could make them rot in a prison, and rue, by bitterness to which that of death is naught, that they had ever laid a profane finger on the treasure of his love; but could their shame, could their dishonour, could their years of darkness and sorrow, atone to him for his loss? Could their chastisement give back to her—his young wife of eighteen, whom he had pressed to his heart so fondly on their first parting—could they give her back the happiness which had but just dawned over her sad youth?

Phyllis had left Saint Brice four hours: that he knew, that and no more. What if she had been waylaid, kidnapped, and been already taken on board the ' Thetis ?' Drops of fear and anguish gathered on his forehead at the thought, and for a moment he stood motionless and powerless with that fatal warning in his hand, the blood flowing feebly and coldly round his heart.

That portion of His Majesty's ships which lay in the neighbouring harbour was then under the rule of the Chevalier de Blangy, an easy old sailor, who listened to every complaint, gave everyone a fair hearing, and thought himself a martyr to duty. "I am a victim," he often said, "a perfect victim." To walk up and down the port, smoking in the sun, was one of the few pleasures this victim enjoyed, and whilst he was thus engaged it was well known that he would heed no complaint, and receive no petitions. Accordingly, when a young man with a blanched face and white lips suddenly stepped before him this afternoon and barred his way, the Chevalier pettishly put his fingers in his ears, and said, angrily: "Not now, sir; in an hour's time I will hear all you have to say, but not now." But the young man, seizing both the Chevalier's arms, compelled his fingers to leave his ears, and with a stern voice and a sterner look, he said :

"I am the Count of Saint Brice. I was married last night to Mademoiselle de la Faille, and this morning my wife was carried off by two Gardes du Pavillon, and forcibly conveyed on board the 'Thetis,' where she is now. I ask to search the ship, and, living or dead, to get my wife back."

The poor Chevalier's pipe fell from his lips, and was broken on the flags as he heard this. A Countess, not a tradesman's wife or daughter, had been abducted by those terrible youths !

"Sir," he said, looking bewildered, "this cannot be. It is impossible."

The Count turned to Gertrude, who stood behind him.

"This woman has been our servant

fifty years. With her own eyes she saw my wife carried away on her way to me; with her own ears she heard her shrieks for help. I ask to search the 'Thetis,' and get her back."

"But the lady may not be on board the 'Thetis,'" cried the Chevalier more and more distressed.

The Count turned to a sailor, and bringing him forward, he said : "This man was waiting for his sweetheart this morning, outside the harbour, when he saw two men and a woman who was weeping bitterly, enter a boat. That woman was my wife. That boat made for the 'Thetis' I ask to search the 'Thetis,' and so get my wife back."

"Sir, that is impossible," desperately said the Chevalier.

"Impossible !" cried the Count whose eyes turned like dark fire. "You tell me that is impossible for me to get my wife back from that den."

"Yes, sir, I do," replied the Chevalier, pointing to the sea. "There is the 'Thetis,' overtake her if you can."

The Count looked towards the far horizon. The sun was setting, the sea was flooded with fire, the sky was one broad sheet of flame, and in that burning glow he saw a black speck. He knew that this speck, which vanished as he looked, was bearing his Phyllis away, that he was powerless to follow, that he might wait years for revenge, that life was wrecked, and that love was lost. Despair conquered him. He clenched his hands, he shook his fist at that pitiless sea, that had helped his ruin, and, with a cry of the sharpest anguish, with a groan of unutterable agony, he sank down senseless on the earth.

The Chevalier was well-nigh distracted. A Countess had been carried off, and her husband, a brave young gentleman, was lying all but dead at his feet. " And what could he do? Why, these awful young men would carry off the Queen of France soon, and everyone came and worried him, and what could he do?"

In the meanwhile Gertrude had her

young master removed to the nearest house, and that careless Nemesis who so often crosses our fate, ordained that the husband of Phyllis should be taken to that old mansion on the port where she had once dwelt, and where, since the death of her mother, and the disappearance of her two sisters, the erring but lovely Manon had lived alone. The poor gentleman was kindly received, and conveyed to the room and laid in the bed with the curtains of faded blue lampas, which Manon had once shared with Phyllis. Without delay the best physician in the town was called in, and when the Count woke, in a terrible fever, from his deadlike swoon, a kind nurse shared with Gertrude the task of tending him day and night.

To some, death comes, after hopeless calamity, a merciful deliverer ; to others, the delirium of illness brings temporary forgetfulness ; but the husband of Phyllis was not so formed. From the first the doctor said he would not die, and though when he woke to life his senses were gone, there remained enough of memory to be his torment. Through all the ravings of fever he remembered that he had lost his Phyllis, and how he had lost her. He went through the search for her over and over again. He followed her from Saint Brice to the château; he tracked her to the city; when he reached it the 'Thetis' was gone. For ever and ever that 'Thetis' was sailing away, robbing him of every happiness and every delight. Fated ship, that had taken all things with it—the tender past, the blissful present, the delightful future! "Thetis! Thetis! how had I wronged you?" he raved, in his delirium, confounding the goddess of dead Olympus with his living enemies. "Give me back my Phyllis." In vain the poor young madman received the tenderest nursing, this silver-footed Thetis killed him by inches. He took poor old Gertrude for her, and kissed her brown hands in pathetic entreaty, with a "Give me back my Phyllis," that was both piteous and despairing. His other nurse, that girl with the blue eyes and the golden hair, he knew but too well.

" Do not come near me," he would say, bending his wrathful eyes upon her; " I know you, and I would rather have Thetis than you. Go away, I say. Go away."

On hearing this harsh sentence the beautiful face would turn away weeping, and after awhile come back, to be again driven away and repulsed sternly. Yet one night the sick man relented.

" I know you are not my Phyllis," he said, " though you are so like her; but cheat me, cheat me—say you are Phyllis."

" I am Phyllis," she replied, softly.

" Then why are you not on board the " Thetis ?' "

" Because I was brought and hidden here till the ' Thetis' sailed."

" And who went away with the ' Thetis ?' "

" Manon ; she took my place. She did it for your sake, and I am your Phyllis. Look."

She bent her face near his; he raised his head eagerly to kiss her, then he pushed her away sternly.

" Where is the mole on your cheek ?" he asked, " that mole which nearly caught me once ! You forget putting it on to-day, my lady. Put it on when you want to cheat me, put it on."

She wept, but he only laughed at her tears. And so it was ever: he either loathed her, and drove her from him, or, when he tolerated her presence, he up-braided her with not cheating him out of his despair.

At length the fever was conquered, delirium left him, and the Count woke back to life, and though not at once, to the bitter memory of his sorrow. His first consciousness was of a room, that could belong neither to Saint Brice nor to the château of La Faille. It was too small for the one, and too dingy for the other. Besides, was not that shipping, which he saw through the open window; were not those tall masts, rising, and white flags fluttering, against the blue sky? As the Count looked thus, the past came back to him in all its agony. He gazed around him, as if to escape from it, and the very image he wanted to fly from, appeared at the foot of his bed, in all its seductive beauty. He uttered a sharp cry, for she stood there before him, weeping and smiling as she wept. She stood there, fair and tender, his wife, his own Phyllis with the mole on her cheek.

" Phyllis, my Phyllis, where have you been all this time ?" he asked, when he could speak.

" Here with you," she answered, gently. " Here all the time with you."

He looked round, as if for some other face. Phyllis shook her head, and said, sadly :

" Manon is gone; I was brought here. She took my place, and went on board the ' Thetis' in my stead. One of the Gardes du Pavillon, who liked her, helped her to cheat the rest. She did it for your sake, and—and she bade me tell you that you were to think of Manon now and then."

" Think of her !" said the Count, much moved. " Ah, surely. How can I but think of one without whom there would have been no more happiness for me ?"

And so these two were happy from that time forth, and the arcadia of their youth dwelt with them for evermore. But if the beautiful Manon was not forgotten by Phyllis and Corydon, she was seen no more by them. A rumour once reached them, in their blissful dream of love, that she had married an old sea captain; but whether it was true or false they never knew. Even in fairy tales, idylls, and romances, some one must go to the wall, some sad Manon must walk in the shade, whilst happy Phyllis and Corydon rejoice in the sun.

The Miller of Manneville.

THE little brackish river which flows through Manneville turns the wheel of many a Norman mill on its way. There is the big mill for the grinding of rape, and which is to become oil in time; there is the tuck-mill, which dyes the river black and blue at certain hours; and there is the flour mill, which belongs to Maître Salomon, and is so picturesque, so green and so lovely, that it is a wonder no painter has found it out as yet.

The river of Manneville is nameless. It springs in a little hollow not far from the road to Fontaine, flows round the village for a mile or so, then glides away with a low plaintive murmur to the sea. Perhaps because its course is so brief, perhaps because it is so soon lost in the great blue waters, it has been allowed to pass through the world without a name. Was it worth while to give any to so short-lived a stream? On one, too, which, being the only river for miles around, could never be mistaken for any other. So the river of Manneville is born, goes on its way, does its good work, and dies unrecorded.

Not far from the dark spot whence it murmurs forth into the bright sunshine, it suddenly spreads into a little lake, skirted with hoary willows and tall beech trees, that cast a deep cool shade on its waters. An old dyke closes one extremity of the lake, and ends in Maître Salomon's mill. Beyond the dyke the lake narrows, and becoming river-like, flows on in the green, fresh shade of fine old trees, till it reaches the village.

But of Manneville, of its street, church,
and houses, there is neither sight nor
sound here. The gray old mill, and its
pleasant stone house and smiling orchard,
ending in a gay flower-garden, are all you
see if you go down to the lake from the
road leading to Fontaine. The picture is
one you never forget, especially if the
wheel of the mill be still. Wherever you
look you see green trees, clear water, and
blue sky, and, closing the scene, the old
mill, seeming to sleep in the sun as if it
were weary of its endless work, and glad
to doze its last days away.

It is not a busy mill. It has had little
corn to grind since the windmill was
built on the hill by Fontaine; but Maitre
Salomon keeps it going; he will not give
in to the windmill; he hates it, talks of
it with cool scorn, and, being a well-to-do
man, he can indulge in his hobby—his
own mill. He likes that mill for many
reasons. His mother was born here, here
she was married, and here she died when
he was a lad of fourteen. Maître Salomon

himself was born at the mill on a midsummer morning, and he is apt to boast that he has never been twenty-four entire hours out of it since that day. Even as the Celestial Empire is the centre of the world to the Chinese, so is his mill the centre of Manneville to Maître Salomon.

Midsummer morning was beautiful and balmy three years ago, and so thought the miller, who was smoking in his orchard, looking at the shadow of the apple trees on the grass, and at the clear sheet of water which rippled gently on the sandy beach at his feet. " I am twenty-nine to-day," he soliloquised. " Well, it is pleasant to live, especially here in the old mill." The young miller did not go beyond this satisfactory conclusion; perhaps because a thrush was singing very sweetly above his head ; perhaps, too, because he rarely vexed his mind with useless speculations. He was a tall young Norman, fair and florid, with happy blue eyes, and a look of calm content on his handsome, good-humoured face which his daily life fulfilled. It was the boast of his cousin and servant, Catherine, that she could do what she pleased with Maitre Salomon, provided she did not disturb his equanimity by speaking of the hateful windmill.

"My dear mother has been dead fifteen years," thought the miller, as a faint sound of church bells came on the summer air. "God rest her soul. She was a good mother to me." And he sighed with the calm sorrow with which we learn to think of the dead.

"Maître Salomon," called out a shrill voice from the house, "will you not go to High Mass to-day?"

"I have been to Low Mass," answered the miller, taking out his pipe.

Catherine was deaf, but taking her master's reply for granted, she pursued: "This is a great holiday. You should go to High Mass, Maitre Salomon."

"I sleep through the sermon," answered the young man, with a cloud on his open face, "and my dear mother used to say,

'Never give scandal in God's church.' And she spoke truly, Catherine; she spoke truly."

But Catherine, who, though deaf, seemed to know all her master's answers by heart, screamed from the house: "And I say you give scandal by staying at home, Maitre Salomon; you give scandal."

This was no doubt unanswerable, for the miller extinguished his pipe, put it in his pocket, and shunning the kitchen, entered the house by a side door, and gently went upstairs to his mother's room. It had never been used since the sad day when she was borne out of it. Such as she had left it after her brief illness, it was still. When the young miller unlocked the door—he always kept the key of that room in his own care—the faint smell of lavender and dried roses which his mother had loved seemed to bring her dear presence back again before him. He closed the door softly—love and death had made the place sacred—and the dim light that stole in through the window, across which a vine had been allowed to fling its broad green boughs, almost unpruned, gave it a solemn and religious aspect.

Maitre Salomon stepped as lightly across the floor as if he feared to waken some sleeper hidden behind the faded pink bed-curtains, all over which were portrayed the fortunes of little Cinderella. He took out his pocket-handkerchief and dusted with it the marble slab of the old chest of drawers. He raised tenderly the blue pin-cushion upon it, and in which his mother's two long silver hair-pins were still stuck, and when he put it down again, he half sighed. Grief was dead, but not that fond regret which never leaves a faithful heart.

"Maître Salomon, I am going," screamed Catherine from the bottom of the stairs.

"Very well," he answered.

"Oh, you are up there again," she muttered, rather indignantly. This room which she was never allowed to enter, unless in her master's presence, was a sore point with Catherine. She disapproved of it, and hinted that it was no better than a calling of ghosts, to be thus keeping up an empty room. " Just ready for them. I wonder you will not go to High Mass to day," she persisted, from the foot of the staircase. " All Manneville will be there : Maitre Pierre Lenud and his pretty wife, Fifine, you know, and Alexis, to whom Annette left that lot of money, and Rénée, the organist's wife. You do not know Rénée, Maitre Salomon."

" We must not go to church to stare at our neighbours and their wives," rather austerely answered the miller ; but he spoke low, and more as if his dead mother could hear the words, than as if they were meant for Catherine.

" And I say it is only a calling of ghosts to keep a room empty for them," she muttered, giving up the point and going her way.

The obstinate miller opened the window. A gentle breeze suddenly stirred the vine-leaves, and a golden sunbeam stole in through a thick cluster, making a warm

light on the red tiled floor. "That vine
must be pruned," thought the miller,
making the opening a little wider with
his hand; he soon paused in sudden surprise at the unexpected picture below him.
This window overlooked the narrowest
part of the river. A tall beech tree that
grew on one bank flung its broad hanging
boughs across the stream to the other
side, and wholly hid its further course and
many windings. The little nook thus
seemingly enclosed was wonderfully cool
and green. There was a cottage close to
it, but it was invisible from the window,
and the only token that the spot was ever
visited by any human being consisted in
two white stepping-stones which had been
placed at the root of the beech tree to
lead from the steep bank down to the
water's edge. Many a time had the miller
seen little birds hopping daintily across
these stones, or dragon flies darting over
the water; but either Susanne, his neighbour, came to fill her pitcher very early or
very late, for never once, often though he

looked out, had he seen her or anyone else by the stream. And now, to his surprise, a young girl, a stranger to Manneville he was sure, stood on the lowest of the stepping-stones, with the water rippling softly over her bare feet. Her curly black hair was loose and hung around her face, which it half hid; the sleeves of her little white bodice were tucked up to her elbows, and left her arms bare, and her faded red cloth petticoat was carefully gathered above her ankles, so as not to get wet. She stood very still, looking down at herself in the water, then suddenly sitting down on the topmost stone, and bending over the river, she took up water in both her hands and began washing her face with great zeal. An obstinate black spot on her left cheek required a good deal of rubbing and several appeals to the natural mirror at her hand, before she was satisfied. Shaking back her hair, she showed the miller a pleasant, round, dimpled face, just then all sparkling with bright waterdrops, and two laughing blue eyes, with an open childish look in them that did one good to see. He thought that, her ablutions being performed, she would go away, but she did not. She wiped her face dry with a white cloth lying on the grass, then took out a little comb from her pocket, and combed out her hair very carefully. Then she tied it back with a crimson ribbon, which she bound round her head after, in what the miller thought, a very becoming fashion; then bending over the water, she looked at herself and seemed by no means to quarrel with her own image.

"Mariette, Mariette, you will never be ready," cried a voice far away.

"I am coming, com—ing," answered the young girl, with a sort of song, and slipping her feet into a pair of wooden shoes that lay by her, she sprang away, and in a moment was hidden from the miller's view. He waited awhile to see if she would return, but she did not, so he let the vine-leaves fall back, closed the window, shut the door, and went down to the solitary kitchen. The sun was shining

through the tall window on the brick
floor, and the great clock was ticking behind the half-open door. The summer
air was still, and as the mill was not at
work, the sound of the church-bells were
very clear. "Catherine is right; I ought
to go to mass," thought the miller; and
as it was not too late, he dressed and
went at once.

High Mass was beginning as Maître
Salomon entered the church of Manneville, and went up to his bench. He had
a whole one to himself, in which he always sat alone. Catherine never used it.
She had sat at the lower end of the church
in a dark corner, and in the draught of
two doors, ever since she was fifteen, and
would have been wretched to sit any-
where else. It was, therefore, with a
start of surprise that the miller saw a
woman kneeling in the seat where, ever
since his mother had died, he had knelt
and prayed alone; and with much trepida-
tion that he recognised the young girl
whom he had seen from the window in his

mother's room. She knelt with her face
buried in her little brown hands, but he was
sure of her identity, and was so disconcerted
that he had barely recovered his presence
of mind by the time the sermon began.
His little neighbour never once turned
towards him. Her eyes were fastened on
the pages of her book and the miller could
scarcely see her bent face. There was
nothing distracting in the top of her white
cap, nor even in the end of the crimson
ribbon which came down behind on her
slender neck; her little girlish figure was
so still that, if his head had not been per-
tinaciously turned her way, Maitre Salomon might have forgotten her presence;
but he did not, and it was only by staring
at the large brass eagle reading-desk
in front of the altar that he succeeded in
keeping his eyes off her till mass was
ended. Even then he kept staring on at
the eagle, till a little voice said in his ear,
" Please, let me pass." Then he gave a
great start, and saw for a moment a little
round face which passed by him, and,

mingling with the crowd, was gone almost
as soon as seen. The miller did not look
for it; he was a shy man by nature and
habit, and went straight home.

Maître Salomon stood on the road in
front of his own house the next day, when
he heard the sound of a beetle hard at
work on some linen in the vicinity of the
beech tree. " It is the little girl with the
red ribbon," thought the miller, and he
went straight up to his mother's room.
He opened the window very softly and
peeped through the vine-leaves; he saw
the little girl with the red ribbon, as he
called her, washing some linen with much
superfluous energy, and a prodigal use
of that noisy beetle which had betrayed
her presence. She knelt in the box lined
with straw which French peasant-women
use for that purpose, and was rinsing out
a long white table-cloth, dyeing the little
river with soap bubbles that floated down
the stream. When this was done, she
sat down on the higher one of the two
stones, and began biting in a piece of

brown bread with the honest appetite of
fifteen.

" It is but a little thing, a young thing,"
thought the miller, watching her with
much pleasure through the vine-leaves.
" How it bites in that hard dry bread,"
and he looked on when the bread was
eaten, and the washing resumed, and he
forgot the passing of time till twelve
struck and the Angelus rang. No sooner
did the little girl hear the church bell
than she started to her feet with a suddenness that partook of alarm, and snatch-
ing up her linen, washed and unwashed,
she rushed off, leaving her box, beetle,
and soap behind her. In a few minutes
Susanne came and fetched them. Then
all was still again, and the little river
flowed on quietly once more, and a white
pigeon alighted on one of the stepping-
stones, and after strutting up and down
across it for awhile, flew away.

" Who and what can she be ?" thought
the miller, as he sat eating his dinner by
the table in the kitchen window. Catherine,

who was washing up plates and dishes by the fireplace, in which, though it was June, a wood fire was crackling, unexpectedly gave him the information he wanted.

"Some people are lucky," began Catherine, in a high, irritated key; "they do not go into service; they have servants of their own, who wear red ribbons in their hair—little pert, conceited things."

The miller, on hearing this, gave Catherine a look which so plainly said "What!" that she resumed in a louder tone: "I say that Susanne's new servant is a scandal! Why she sat in your bench yesterday, Maître Salomon! She is as saucy as a sparrow. I saw her washing this morning; and how Susanne can trust her with linen—why a baby knows as much about washing as she does, with her red ribbon. A little gadder too! Why, when twelve struck, instead of seeing to her mistress's dinner, and turning her hand to anything useful, she rushed past our garden with her head bare and her arms all covered with soap-suds, and her feet almost out of her wooden shoes, and ran along like a mad thing on the road to Fontaine. Susanne must be crazy to have taken that little thing, with as much sense in her head as a linnet. And her name is Mariette, too," she added, as if this were the culminating point in the sins of Susanne's servant.

The miller heard this, but all he thought was: " Why did she start off so as twelve struck, and what could she be racing off to Fontaine for ?" and instead of smoking his after-dinner pipe by the little lake as usual, he went and walked up and down the hedge that divides his garden from the road. Presently he heard a clatter of wooden shoes, and looking over the hedge, the tall miller saw a little figure coming towards him. It was she, bare-headed, and dressed just as he had seen her washing, in a dingy old red petticoat, and with a large cotton handkerchief loosely fastened around her neck. She was much flushed, and rather out of breath, but she brought back neither bundle nor basket. The miller looked after her as she dived down the shady path that led to Susanne's cottage, and he wondered what her errand on that lonely sunburnt road had been.

Maître Salomon had not much to do about this time, so he went up and down a good deal to his mother's room, or walked in his garden by the hedge, but he did not see Mariette. Once or twice, however, he heârd her singing in a voice so sweet and clear that he thought, " Catherine was right in calling her a linnet. She is a bird, one hears but does not see her."

At length, on the Saturday morning, he saw her again from behind the vine-leaves. She had come for water to the river, and laying her pitcher slantwise in the stream, she let it fill there slowly, idly watching the water as it flowed in and out. She stood in the dry shade of the beech tree, but here and there a sunbeam stole in upon her, and one played on her head and lit up her dark hair with specks of the richest gold. The miller—who perhaps had a painter's eye—was watching her with infinite pleasure, when the noonday Angelus rang. On hearing it, Mariette snatched up her pitcher, which was not half full, and darted away, leaving a great blank of shade on the spot where she had been.

The miller went down to the kitchen, took his hat from its peg behind the door, and without heeding Catherine's "Why, Maitre Salomon, the soup is on table," he walked out on the road to Fontaine. To his surprise he saw Mariette climbing up a narrow path leading to a shady orchard on the left side of the road, and which belonged to no less a person than the miller himself. What could take her there? It was a wild, secluded spot, beyond which extended many a cornfield, and where the miller's cow grazed alone all the day long. "She cannot want to talk with Roquette," thought the miller, "and surely my unripe apples cannot tempt her." And he too climbed up the path, and was soon

straying among the low, broad apple-
trees. The spot was wild and lovely, a
little nest of green lying in the hollow lap
of the hill. Roquette was grazing there
in solitary state, and a swarm of wild
bees that had made its nest in a hollow
tree, filled the place with a soft drowsy
murmur, very pleasant to hear in the hot
summer noon; lovely wild flowers and
large white mushrooms also grew there in
abundance, and lent their wild beauty to
the miller's orchard; but the little brown-
headed girl whom he had followed there
was invisible. At length he found her
out. The southern end of the orchard
was enclosed by a bank of mossy rock and
green earth, at the foot of which grew a
lonely oak, young and strong and with
sturdy boughs, that flung their shade far
into the neighbouring cornfield. Now
Mariette was perched bird-like on the
lowest of these boughs, and whilst she
clung with one arm to the trunk of the
oak, she shaded her eyes with the hand
that was free, looking earnestly at some-

thing far away. Suddenly she dropped
down as lightly from her bough as if she
had had a pair of wings to her back, and
skipping among the rocks of the bank,
she ran away through the orchard, and
passed close to the miller, looking up at
him with childish, fearless eyes, and
giving him a little nod as he stepped aside
to make way for her. Maître Salomon
looked after her till she had vanished,
then he climbed up the bank, and without
requiring the aid of the oak bough, he
scanned attentively the prospect at which
Mariette had been gazing. Corn, tall
yellow corn, corn waving beneath the
summer sun in the soft summer air, was
all he saw—save far away in the glittering
haze of noonday, the sails of the windmill
moving lazily. Even as the miller eyed
them askance their motion ceased, and all
was still again in the tranquil landscape.
" It never can be to look at that thing,
that she came here," thought the miller ;
" she knows better, I am sure, little
though she is."

However that might be, close observation gave the miller the certainty that every day a little before noon Mariette went up to his orchard. Only once did he follow her and watch her from a distance, and then he saw her again perched in the tree. " I suppose it is a bird, and likes that," thought the miller, greatly puzzled.

Every village has its bad character. The bad character of Manneville just then was a young scamp called Simon Petit, who, though no more than ten years old, had the credit of robbing all the farm-yards and plundering all the orchards in the place. A favourite exploit of this young brigand's was also to catch, in spite of every penal injunction to the contrary, the speckled trout that played on the pretty bed of the little river.

" The young villain is at his old tricks," indignantly thought Maitre Salomon, as looking through the vine-leaves on a sunny morning, he saw, instead of Mariette, the little cunning face and serpent figure of Simon, who, armed with a long pole, was cautiously exploring the banks of the river. He stole away, and was soon hidden among the alder bushes. He had scarcely vanished, when Mariette appeared with a pitcher in her hand. She laid it down in the stream, and watched the water flowing into it, with a sad, dejected look. Twelve struck; Mariette did not stir. Something had happened assuredly, or she would never stand thus with downcast eyes and arms hanging down loosely by her side. But suddenly she gave a start as Simon Petit, stepping out from behind the alder bushes, appeared before her with a fine trout in his hand. He, too, was taken by surprise, but looking her boldly in the face, he said with cool effrontery :—

"The trout jumped out of the river, and so I picked it up. You saw it jumping, did you not?"

"No, indeed," bluntly answered Mariette. She looked incredulous; Simon's little cunning eyes winked, but he was mute. Mariette said: "Do something for me, and no one shall know about the trout; run up the road, go through the orchard on the left hand, climb up into the oak tree, and tell me if the sails of the windmill are quiet or turning?"

" What do you want to know that for?" asked Simon.

" Never mind."

" Then why do you not go yourself?"

" Will you go or not?" she asked, stamping her foot impatiently.

She held out no threat about the trout, yet Simon gave in at once, and promising to do her errand, he vanished. Mariette sat down on the higher of the two stepping-stones, and clasping her hands around her knees, waited patiently for his return.

Maître Salomon, shaking his head at what he had heard and seen, went down stairs, walked out on the road, and found Simon there, peering round him before he ventured into the orchard, for he had been caught there once upon a time, and fear, like a dragon, kept watch in the path. The miller had no need to speak. The moment Simon saw him, he caught up his trout, which he had hidden in a cool hollow of the hedge, and fled precipitately. The miller looked after him with grim satisfaction, and thought: "I suppose I must do that little thing's errand, and see about that windmill myself now."

So he went up to his orchard and ascertained that his enemy the windmill was motionless. "But what can she want to know that for?" thought Maître Salomon as he came down again.

"Why your soup has been cooling this half hour, Maître Salomon," cried Catherine, standing on the threshold of the kitchen door; but without heeding her, Maitre Salomon walked round the mill, took a little path that led to the river, and found Mariette still sitting on the stepping-stone and waiting there for Simon's return. She looked round on hearing the miller's step, and gazed up at him with simple wonder on her young face. He

looked down at her quietly, and entered
at once on his subject. " I am the miller,
and yonder is my mill, and from my window, the one with the vine-leaves up
there, I heard you a while ago talking to
that good-for-nothing Simon Petit. Take
my advice, and have nothing to do with
that fellow, who has more wickedness in
his little finger than many a big man in
his whole body."

" And is there a window up there behind the vine?" was Mariette's only reply.
" Well, I should never have thought so;
how can you see from behind these thick
green leaves?"

" That is neither here nor there," answered the miller, a little impatiently;
" but Simon knows better than to put a
foot in my orchard since the day when I
caught him stoning Roquette after filling
his cap with apples; so he ran away when
he saw me. Being, as it were, the cause
of your disappointment, I went in his
stead, though what you can want to look
at that windmill for, is more than I can

imagine. Take my word for it, of all the
ugly things of man's making, a windmill
is the ugliest, and *that* windmill is the
ugliest I ever saw. But every one to his
liking ; and any time you fancy going up
to the orchard, why do so, and take some
of the fruit and be welcome to it, for you
see the orchard is mine, and if I make
you welcome, why no one has a right to
gainsay it."

"Thank you," replied Mariette, who
looked as if she had not minded a word
he was uttering. "But please, were the
sails going ?"

"Why should they be ?" asked the
miller rather sharply. "I tell you that
mill is a bad thing altogether, and that he
who built it has rued it many and many a
time."

"Well, but were the sails going ?" again
asked Mariette, looking anxious.

"No !" decisively answered the miller ;
"they were as still as if they were
nailed."

The colour fled from Mariette's cheeks,
and left them white.

"They were not going," she said faintly; "then I am undone, undone!" and she looked at him so wildly, wringing her hands, thăt the miller thought she was surely distracted.

"Why, child," he argued, "what can that windmill be to you?"

Mariette did not answer him; but looking at him in the same wild way, she rose and left him without uttering another word. "Is the little thing crazy?" thought Maître Salomon, going back to the mill-house a strangely puzzled man.

This was to be a day of events to every one about the mill: Catherine, much perplexed by Maître Salomon's fancy to go out instead of eating his soup, was stealing out softly to see what he was about when she was accosted by an old beggar-woman from Fontaine, named Justine.

"This is not Friday," said Catherine, sharply, "come on Friday, and you will get something, as usual." Friday is the great begging and almsgiving day in Manneville.

"You should not let riches harden your heart, Mademoiselle Catherine," said Justine pitifully. "You should not. It is not because your cousin Médéric has left you all that money that you should ill-use the poor, Mademoiselle Catherine."

Even the deaf can hear the magic words "riches" and "money." Catherine put questions and was answered, and Catherine learned with indignation and dismay that her cousin, Maître Médéric, the childless widower, was dead and buried, and that his heirs had begun to quarrel over his inheritance, without thinking it needful to summon her to a division of the spoil. Catherine was a woman of spirit. In five minutes her resolve was taken, and when Maitre Salomon came in to his dinner, Catherine, instead of giving him a scolding, informed him, in her highest key, that she was going to Fontaine to get her rights; that she was sure the old oaken press, black and bright as ebony, would be gone if she delayed; and last of all that her cousin Médéric was dead.

Thus it happened that Maitre Salomon, instead of being cheered by the conversation of Catherine that evening, sat alone in his kitchen, and after eating his supper of bread and cheese, and drinking his glass of cider, looked dreamily in the embers of his decaying fire of rape stalks.

The evenings are always chill in Manneville, and this was a rainy one; besides, Maitre Salomon liked company, "and fire is good company at any time, as my mother used to say," he remarked to himself. So he sat, and was looking absently at the mild red glow on his hearth, when the kitchen door behind him opened softly, and, looking sharply round, the miller saw the pale, startled face of Mariette in the opening.

" Oh, please, can I come in ?" she whispered. " I shall stay only a little while ; but please do let me in."

" Come in," said the miller, rising. " What is it ?"

Mariette, instead of answering him, darted in, looked round her sharply, espied, spite the mild gloom in the kitchen, the door that led to the rooms on the first floor, and opening it, flew up the steps, as swift and light as a kitten. The miller was rather bewildered, but phlegmatic people rarely lose their presence of mind; so Maitre Salomon lit a candle, bolted the kitchen door, and followed his visitor, whom he found on the landing hiding behind the door of Catherine's room.

" Mariette," he said, " what has happened ?"

" The tinker has come for me," she replied pitifully. " He says he is my father you know; but I know he is not, and I will never go away with him, never. He came into Susanne's, but I jumped out of the window as he entered the door, and pray do not tell him I am here, for I hate him, I do."

The light of the miller's candle fell on the pale, tearful face of the frightened girl.

" The tinker—what tinker ?" he asked.

" The tinker," she said pettishly, as if the world held but one, " and I hate him, and do not tell him I am here; and pray do not give me up to him."

If she had been an outcast, steeped in shame and sin, the miller could not have resisted the appeal nor the pitiful look she raised to his.

" No one shall touch thee here," he said, almost sternly. "And look," he added, drawing a key from his pocket and opening a door at the furthest end of the landing, "this is my dead mother's room. Take the light, go in, and lock the door on thyself, and let us see who will go in after thee there."

Mariette did as she was bid, and entered the room in a silent awe, wakened by the words "dead mother." The miller waited till she had locked the door on herself, then he went downstairs, lit another candle, unbolted the door, and taking out his pipe, began to smoke leisurely. He had not been engaged thus five minutes when the door opened, and Catherine, followed by the dirtiest and most ill-looking gipsy sort of tinker whom the miller had ever set his eyes on, entered the kitchen.

"Well, Maître Salomon," she cried in breathless indignation, "I told you how it would be. The black oaken press was gone, and the warming-pan as well. That warming-pan had been a hundred years in the family, and I had a longing for it ever since I was a child. You could read seventeen hundred and fifty-five upon it quite plainly, and this honest tinker whom I have just met, actually had it yesterday from my cousin Angélique herself to clean up, and he says it was as good as new and as bright as gold."

"It was a noble warming-pan," said the tinker, in a hollow voice, whilst his dark eye stole about the room as if in search of something or some one. He had a swarthy face, harsh features, and a rusty brown beard, and the miller thought he had never seen so evil-looking a fellow; so, being a man of few words, he asked shortly, "What is your business here?"

"I came about some saucepans," humbly answered the tinker, looking at Catherine.

"Yes, you shall have them all," she replied, guessing what was going on, " but I must know what Angélique got besides the warming pan : I know Médéric had copper saucepans; there was one as large as this—suppose you begin with it?"

She was going to take down a large casserole, and the tinker was stepping forward to take it from her, when the miller took out his pipe, stretched out his arm, and uttered a "Stop," so loud and imperative that even Catherine heard it.

"Not a casserole, not a warming-pan of my late mother's, shall that man touch," he said sternly. "Such as they are now, they remain."

Having uttered this sentence with due solemnity, the miller rose and walked out. Catherine was sure to understand that when the miller walked out of his own kitchen he had invariably pronounced some sentence from which there was no appeal.

Maitre Salomon went no farther than
the end of his own garden. He suddenly
remembered that he had left the enemy in
the very heart of the citadel, and walking
back to the house at once, he found the
kitchen empty, whilst a streak of light
coming down the staircase, and a sound
of voices, guided him to the first floor.
He walked up softly, and caught the
tinker in the act of trying the door of his
mother's room, whilst he was saying, " I
dare say she is in here."

Maitre Salomon took the gipsy by the
arm, swung him round, and thrusting
him down stairs, exclaimed in wrath, very
unusual to him, " You scoundrel, how
dare you attempt to go in there? And
you, Catherine, are you mad, and do you
mean us to part, that you brought him
up here?"

" Heaven bless you ! Maitre Salomon,"
cried Catherine, looking frightened out of
her wits, " the poor man meant no harm,
and knew nothing about the room. He
is only looking after his cat, Minette. It

seems she escaped from him a while ago,
so I dare say he thought she had crept up
the vine and got in there, and I hope you
have not hurt the honest man. He seems
so fond of his cat; I suppose he carries
her about with him; and how was he to
know that doors are locked, and rooms
kept for ghosts, poor man."

Without heeding this speech, the miller
went down and ascertained that the in-
truder was gone; but when Catherine,
after casting this parting taunt about
ghosts and the closed door, came down in
her turn and looked about her, she saw,
to her dismay, that her new umbrella,
which she had put in a corner on coming
in, had disappeared as well as the tinker.

"The honest man took it to clean it up
for you," said the miller, with grim satisfaction. "Perhaps he thought it was
Minette."

"The thief! I shall catch him yet,"
cried Catherine. But the tinker, whether
a thief or not, was not so easily caught;
and when at the end of ten minutes she

came back red with anger and running, she bore no umbrella in her hand. Her lamentations at this calamitous ending of her journey to Fontaine in search of an inheritance were so loud and so trouble-some, that the miller said impatiently, "Go to bed, Catherine, go to bed, and let us hear no more about the umbrella or the tinker."

And as Catherine was tired, she did go to bed after a while, not without grum-ling at the hard-heartedness of men, for whom one might slave and slave, and be treated like a dog in the end.

Maître Salomon bore all this philosophi-cally; and when the house was quiet once more, he went to the dresser, took down a plate, put bread and cheese on the table, and filled a jug with cider. Then he softly stole upstairs, and tapped at the door of his mother's room. It opened cautiously, and Mariette's little round face and startled eyes peeped out at last.

"You may come down," said the miller; "he is gone. Catherine is in bed, and she is deaf as a post."

Mariette obeyed, not without casting many startled looks around her.

"I tell you not to be afraid," said the miller, when they stood in the kitchen. "He is gone, and here are bread and cheese and cider for you. Eat and drink; you are as pale as a ghost."

At first Mariette would not hear of eating or drinking, and kept looking behind her back; but when the miller bolted the door, she uttered a sigh of relief, sat down, and after a little coaxing, took a sip of the cider; then, after a little more persuasion, she began to bite in the bread and cheese, remarking, apologetically:

"I was just sitting down to supper when he came in at the door, and I had to jump out of the window."

The miller looked at her fresh young face, and remembering the sallow, ill-looking tinker, he could not help saying: "Surely that fellow is no father of yours?"

But Mariette raised her eyebrows, pursed up her lips, and shaking her head wisely, said, "She did not know—she could not tell. He might not be her father; but then she remembered no other. He used to beat her, to be sure; but some fathers beat their daughters. All she remembered of herself was trotting by his side when he went about tinkering, and being sometimes carried on his back; of course he made her beg, but she did not get much; may be that was why he beat her. Perhaps he had stolen her, and that she was some grand lady's offspring. Only how could she tell? It is so hard to know whose child one is," argued Mariette, gravely. "It was because he beat her so one evening that Père Joseph, who built the windmill, you know, that handsome windmill"—Maitre Salomon winced— "bought her from the tinker through sheer pity, and that was how she had been living with Jacques in the windmill ever since dear Père Joseph died." As she came to this part of her story Mariette's eyes grew dim, and her voice faltered. The miller looked hard at her, and was silent awhile.

"I suppose you are to marry Jacques, and live in that handsome windmill," he remarked, rather shortly.

"Marry Jacques! Why Jacques was married," pettishly exclaimed Mariette. "As to living in the windmill, how could she, when she was pursued by that horrid tinker? Had she not been obliged to come and hide from him at Susanne's? And had it not been agreed between her and Jacques that he would use the sails of his windmill as a signal to let her know when the tinker was coming? And had not Jacques sent her word that very morning not to stir out of doors? And was she not ready to expire with sheer fright when Maitre Salomon told her that the sails of the windmill were motionless, and she thereby knew that the dreadful tinker was on her track? But she would die first, she would, before she went again with him tramping about the country, mending old saucepans. Yes, she would die first; but what a pretty room that was upstairs, only how terrified she was in it, but then the story of Cinderella on the curtains, was so pretty that she could not help looking at it, and reading the legends under every picture: she had never seen such a pretty room." And so she prattled on, eating and drinking all the time, and seeming to have put by every fear and every care.

Many a time had the miller shaken his head as he listened to her story. It was such a pitiful one. He saw her a little child, wandering about with that savage tinker, beaten, ill-used, made to beg, and only saved from his clutches by becoming a dependent in a stranger's house. They had been kind to her, it seemed, at the windmill, but this Jacques had not married her, of course not, and what was to become of her now, poor little thoughtless thing?

"Mariette," he said at length, "hast thou got a sweetheart?"

"No," replied Mariette, shortly.

"No lad, no young man of Fontaine, whom thou wouldst care for and like to marry?"

" Where is the use, when no one would have me ?" she said, impatiently.

" Then she did care for some one," thought the miller, a little downcast; but no, a few more questions convinced him that Mariette was fancy free, only she knew very well that because of her doubtful birth and poverty no one would care to have her, and it did not please her to be reminded of the fact.

" Well, well, there is time enough for thee to enter on the cares of marriage," said the miller; " yet it would save thee from the tinker. Only just promise me this—do not marry without letting me know about it first ?"

" Why so ?" asked Mariette, opening her blue eyes.

" I may want to make thee a present," replied the miller, after a long pause.

Mariette looked grateful and beaming; but all of a sudden the look of fear came back to her face. She had heard a noise outside; she was sure the tinker was coming. In vain the miller reminded her that the tinker having taken Catherine's umbrella, would not come back. Mariette assured him that to steal and to return to the very house whence he had stolen was the tinker's way. In short, she was so frightened and so restless that Maître Salomon, struck with a bright idea, or what he thought such, said:

" Do not leave the house for fear thou shouldst meet the tinker, child. Go back to the room upstairs, and sleep there for to-night. It is my mother's room, and no one has slept in it since she died. I will walk round to Susanne, and tell her that thou art safe here."

Mariette looked charmed, then frightened. Security is delightful; but ghosts are dreadful company, and Catherine's words about that room had not fallen on heedless ears; but ghosts, after all, are not so terrible as the living, so she accepted the miller's hospitable proposal, and whilst he went round to tell Susanne of her whereabouts, Mariette stole back to her refuge upstairs.

She was not very timorous, after all; and, although she entered that room with a sort of awe, it soon gave place to other feelings. She liked the scent of the lavender and dried roses; she liked those pink bed-curtains, and the story of little Cinderella upon them; so noble a chest of drawers as this she had never seen; and the faded blue pincushion, with the long silver pins in it, was a marvel in her eyes. Not in all the windmill was there a room like this! Surely the late owner of that room had been a happy woman? Was she like her son, wondered Mariette, tall and fair, and had she blue eyes and a serious smile? As she stood on the middle of the floor, looking round her, with a light in her hand, and thus speculating, she suddenly thought of something else, put down the light, went to the window, and, opening it softly, and parting the vine-leaves, looked out on the dark night.

It was not all dark, for the moon was

out, riding in the sky with strange haste, thought Mariette. Her light fell in, streaks on the little gurgling river below, making patches of silver here and there. Everything was very still : then, all of a sudden, Mariette heard voices talking low in that stillness. One was Susanne's, and the other—yes, she was sure the other voice was the tinker's. What was he saying? She could not tell, for terror almost paralysed her, but she could guess, for she heard the words " room" and " vine-leaves" very plainly. Had the light betrayed her? Mariette ran and blew it out at once, then came back to the window, and, not daring to put her head out through the vine leaves, keeping in her breath, so great were her terror and her wish to hear more, she listened intently, whilst the careless moon still rode in the sky, throwing her quivering light on the little river gliding softly on its way to the sea.

Susanne was not in her cottage when Maitre Salomon went to tell her that

Mariette was at the mill-house. He went again in an hour's time, but Susanne had not returned ; he shook her door, and knocked at it again. "Well, the child is safe, at least," thought the miller, and he went back to his own home, and, after sitting up till midnight—a very rare occurrence with him—he softly went upstairs to bed. He paused as he passed by the door of his mother's room. It was very still. "The little bird is fast asleep," he thought kindly. "It has put its head under its wing after all its troubles, and it is fast asleep." And he felt hospitably glad to have given this poor hunted bird so safe a nest.

Catherine, whose slumbers had been much disturbed by dreams of the black oaken press, the warming pan, and her stolen umbrella, rose with dawn, and was rather surprised to find her master below with a loaf and a plateful of freshly gathered cherries on the table before him. "Are you hungry, Maitre Salomon," she exclaimed. "Why you never eat at this hour!"

"I suppose I can eat my own cherries when I like," he answered shortly; and to put an end to her questions he walked out into the garden. He felt annoyed not to have been beforehand with Catherine; he was sure Mariette was awake and hungry, and he wished her to eat some of his cherries, the best in Manneville; also he had been thinking all night over something which he wished to say to her this morning. For one so calm, not to say phlegmatic, Maître Salomon felt in a rare fever, and there was a great throb of mingled uneasiness and joy at his heart, when he saw Catherine leave the house, and heard her scream to him from the garden gate that she was going to look for her umbrella, and would not be long away.

"She is always long, God bless her poor soul!" thought Maitre Salomon, going back to the house. His first act was to bolt the kitchen door, so as not to be surprised, then he stole upstairs, and knocking softly at the door of his mother's room, he said aloud: "Mariette, Catherine is gone, and thou must have something to eat. Shall I bring thee the bread and cherries, and leave them at the door, or wilt thou come down to the kitchen. It is nice and cool, and the door is bolted." Mariette returned no answer.

Was she still asleep? These young things sleep both sound and late. The miller raised his voice and spoke again— in vain. With a vague suspicion of the truth, he tried the door, it yielded to his hand. He looked in from the threshold; Mariette was not there. The bed had not been slept in, the window was open, the cage was empty, and the bird was flown. She had fled in the night through the door, or down the window, by the help of the old vine; no matter when or how, one thing was certain, she was gone—gone without so much as bidding him good-bye, or saying " I thank you."

She was an ungrateful child, and the miller felt he ought not to have given her another thought; but he could not help himself, and even though he felt sure he

should not find her at Susanne's, he yet
went round at once to his neighbour's cottage. Susanne's amazement at his questions was too genuine to be feigned. She
had seen nothing of the girl since she had
left her cottage the evening before.

"I dare say the tinker has got her, after
all," said Susanne, shaking her head; "I
always said he would. He is her father,
you know."

How calmly she spoke of it. Maitre
Salomon felt too angry to do more than
turn his back upon her and walk away.
He did not go back to his own house.
He felt sadly sure that he should be as
unsuccessful in Fontaine as he had been
with Susanne; yet a tormenting power
which he could not resist actually made
him walk off at once to that object of his
aversion the windmill, and seek the fugi-
tive there. "I only want to know that
she is safe, that is all," he said to himself,
as if he needed that justification of his
egregious piece of folly. "She is a child,
and she slept, or was to sleep, in my

mother's room, and so I ought to know what has become of her."

Maitre Salomon found the miller, a sturdy young man white with flour, standing at his own door with a fat baby in his arms. "I come to see about Mariette," said Maître Salomon abruptly; for the sight of the windmill and of his rival had roused his old animosity to all its early vigour. "I think she ought not to have gone away without bidding me good-bye; but that is neither here nor there; provided she is safe, I am content; let her be civil or not."

"Marie," called the miller, "come out. Here is the miller from Manneville, who has something to say about Mariette." A fresh young woman came out on this summons, and Maitre Salomon telling them both briefly all he knew, again asked about Mariette.

"Then the tinker has got her, after all," said the young miller coolly. "Marie, take the baby, it is getting sleepy." Then turning to Maitre Salomon: "You know nothing more about her, I suppose?"

"Did I not come to ask about her?" said the miller, curtly.

"Ah! to be sure." And, having handed the baby to his wife, the owner of the windmill looked hard at the owner of the watermill. Maitre Salomon felt exasperated.

"Will you do nothing? Will you not interfere?" he asked, glaring at his enemy.

"I am that baby's father, and the tinker is Mariette's father," stolidly answered Jacques.

"I do not believe it. I will never believe the wretch is that poor innocent child's father!" indignantly retorted Maitre Salomon.

"Perhaps he is not," quietly said Jacques, and he looked at his rival as much as to say: "If you please, that matter is settled."

Maître Salomon scorned to waste any more words on this unfeeling animal. With a sad and heavy heart he went home, thinking all the way: "Oh, Mariette; if

I had had the care of you all these years,
I would not let you go so coolly from me;
and no tinker, not were he ten times your
father, should have taken you."

Maître Salomon found Catherine at
home, and in great glee. "I have found
my umbrella," she cried. "The villain
had sold it to Victoire, but I made her
give it back; and he is in prison at Fontaine, the good-for-nothing scapegrace, for
having stolen Désiré's new chaldron, which
he bought last Michaelmas, you know."

"In prison at Fontaine," cried the miller, with sudden hope, "and—and was
anyone found with him?"

Joy seemed to have opened Catherine's
ears, for she heard and answered the question. "Some one with him? No, indeed;
there is a band of them, no doubt; but he
was caught alone."

The miller was glad to think the child
was safe; but it stung him to learn that
she had not been forcibly taken away.
"It was of her own free will that she left
me so ungratefully in the night," he

thought, sitting down with a downcast look. " She wanted me no more, and so she stole away without so much as ' good-bye ' or ' thank you,' little uncivil thing. I will think no more about her."

" Why, Maître Salomon, you have not eaten your cherries, after all," said Catherine.

" Eat them, Catherine, or give them away," he replied, with a sorrowful shake of his head ; " I want no cherries."

He rose and went upstairs as he said it. Catherine ate half the cherries and gave the rest to a neighbour's child, whilst Maitre Salomon locked the door of his mother's room and said to himself, as he put the key in his pocket, " That is the end of my fancy ! yes, that is the end."

There was an epidemic in Manneville about this time, and Maitre Salomon proved one of its first victims. He did not die, indeed, as his neighbour Susanne did, but he lay ill for many weeks, and when he recovered Catherine took the disease, and lay in her grave before ten days were

over. She had been years with her young
cousin and master, and though she was
deaf and wilful, not to say tiresome, he
missed her much, and grieved for her sin-
cerely.

" You must take some one else, Maître
Salomon," said his female neighbours.
" Take little Catherine : her having the
name you are so used to, will make it con-
venient."

" Take Lunie," said another, " she is as
good a worker as you can get."

" Time enough for it all," gloomily replied the miller, evidently wishing to be left
to his own ways. These were dull and sad
enough. It might be his recent illness ; it
might be the death of Catherine ; it might
be anything else, but life certainly was
very joyless to Maitre Salomon just then.
Even his mill had ceased to please him ;
even his mother's room he rarely entered
now ; and he must have been a very touchy
man, for he was always brooding over
Mariette's want of civility. " I had not
deserved it from her," he said to himself,

as he sat alone one evening indulging in retrospective discontent, "and I am sure she was hiding in the windmill all the time I was talking to that Jacques of hers. Of course she was laughing at me to be running after her like a fool. And I had been kind to her, and if my mother had taken her, I am sure she would, poor, dear soul, if she had had the opportunity. Mariette would have found a difference between the watermill of Manneville and the windmill of Fontaine."

A great difference the young miller's fancy certainly made in Mariette's imaginary destiny at the watermill. He played with her as a child in the garden, and on the banks of the little lake; he took her up to his mother's room and made her look out on the river from behind the vine; he brought her home some of the smartest of red ribbons for her dark hair as she grew up, and enjoyed her bright eyes and merry laugh, when he took these ribbons out of his pocket and held them up to her admiration; and above all he allowed no Marie and no fat baby to come between him and his little friend. As for the tinker, he disposed of him by making him confess, through the might of some irresistible argument, that Mariette was no child of his, but an orphan whom he had stolen, and whose relations were all dead. Thus far had the miller's reverie proceeded, when a tap at his kitchen door roused him. "Here they are, coming again to worry me about little Catherine and Lunie," he thought, annoyed at being disturbed at that particular part of his dream : and though he said "Come in," he did not look round.

The door opened gently, a light step crossed the kitchen floor, and drew near him. Then the miller looked up, and in the dim twilight he saw Mariette herself standing before him with only the kitchen table, by which he sat, between them. He was so amazed at this unexpected apparition that he could not speak.

"I am afraid you are angry with me," timidly said Mariette, "but I could not help running away that night. I heard

the tinker talking to Susanne, and when
he came round to the mill-house door I
was so frightened that I jumped out of
the window and nearly got drowned. I ran
away to the windmill, and have been hiding
ever since: but I am safe now, for he is
in prison for three years, and I am so glad;
and I hope you are not angry with me."

"I am not," replied the miller, slowly;
"but it was not civil to run away, Mademoiselle Mariette."

Mariette hung her head abashed, and was
mute; then, suddenly looking up and speaking in a rapid, childish way, "I do not
come for the present, Maître Salomon; I
do not want it; but I had promised to
tell you, and I am going to get married.
Jacques and Marie have found me a husband—Marie's cousin. They did not want
me to tell you, but I said I had promised;
and I am to be married next week."

"Married?" repeated the miller, staring
at her, "married, and you come and tell
me."

"Yes I had promised, Maître Salomon.
Have you forgotten?"

He could not answer. He still stared at her as she stood there before him, neat, demure, and pretty, a little bird-like creature, and he asked himself, with a sharp pang, why he could not have had her as well as another man.

"Married!" he said again, setting his teeth as he spoke: " why, what makes you marry ?"

Mariette stared in her turn. Had he forgotten the advice he had given her to marry, in order to be safe from the tinker ? Why, she had repeated this advice to Jacques, and he had thought so well of it, that he and Marie had found her a husband.

" Do not tell me that again," interrupted the miller, exasperated. " Of course you like him !"

" Not much," replied Mariette, confidentially; " he is old; fifty, at least."

" Fifty ! Why, he could be your grandfather," exclaimed Maitre Salomon.

" He is very grey as well," resumed Mariette, looking depressed; "and he is deaf of one ear, but he hears very well with the other, and I like his eldest daughter, Louise, so much."

So this man was not merely old, deaf, and grey, but he was also a widower. Was he rich, at least, to make up for so many drawbacks? asked the miller, indignantly.

" Rich !" echoed Mariette, with a gay laugh, " if he were rich he would not have me. But Louise is going to get married, and he wants some one to take care of him, and Jacques wants me to be safe from the tinker, so he and Marie found him out. He was not willing at first, but he made up his mind and came and said so this morning, and we are to be married next week."

Maitre Salomon could not believe his ears. Was she, this pretty, innocent, thoughtless child, to be sacrificed so? Was she to become an old man's nurse in order to be saved from a tinker who was not her father, Maitre Salomon was sure. He rose, he walked about his kitchen in great agitation; he came back at last to Mariette, and with a great tightening at his throat, said : " Mariette, they all tell me to take

some one instead of Catherine, but the fact
is I feel I want a wife. Do you know of
one that would suit me ?"

" Oh, so well," cried Mariette, bright-
ening; " there is Jacques' sister Delphine;
she is pretty, and has plenty of money,
and——"

" That was not what I meant to say,"
interrupted Maître Salomon, reddening;
" the fact is I cannot bear to see you
marry that deaf old widower, who could
not make up his mind—no, that is not it
either; the truth is, Mariette," exclaimed
the miller, desperately, "that I took a
fancy to you when I saw you from behind
the vine-leaves in my mother's room,
washing your face and combing your hair,
and if you will just throw the old fellow
over and have me, why we can get married, and you can come here at once:
because you see," added Maître Salomon,
who could not help being a matter-of-fact
Norman, " everything is going wrong
since Catherine died, and the neighbours

worry my life out about Lunie and little Catherine, they do."

Mariette heard him, but thought she was dreaming. Could the miller, the handsome, rich young miller of Manneville be in earnest or was *he* dreaming, that he talked so. "Well!" said Maitre Salomon, who stood before her looking down in her face.

"You cannot mean it," she replied, looking up at him with evident doubt in her blue eyes. "It is too good to be true."

But it was not too good to be true, after all, and Mariette, half laughing, half crying for joy, could not help saying, "Oh, I am so glad—so glad! for I could not bear him, only I was so frightened of the tinker. And he squints, you know," she added, confidentially; "but I did not like to say so."

The miller was a man of few words, and his courting, for many reasons, was a brief one. Marie was very much affronted that her cousin should be so cavalierly jilted; but Jacques, who had never liked the match, chuckled at its being broken off with such evident enjoyment that he won the heart of Maitre Salomon, who actually ceased to think the windmill the ugliest he had ever seen.

Mariette made the best of millers' wives. She sang like a lark, was as busy as a bee, and thought nothing and no one could compare with the mill and the Miller of Manneville. Every one liked her; even the neighbours, who had recommended Lunie and little Catherine, said she was not amiss. She had but one fault; she was too fond of looking out of that window with the vine-leaves growing so thick and green around it, and whence you can see the stepping-stones and the tall beech tree, and the little shining river flowing on in golden sunlight or green shade.

The tinker died in prison, and had no time to say anything about Mariette's relations. "Never mind," says Maître Salomon, "I am sure they are all dead."

Rénée.

THE road from Manneville to Fontaine is very beautiful, but it is also very lonely. On either side of it grow tall oaks, between which you see soft green slopes, where cows are grazing quietly on broad fields, full of yellow waving corn; but neither farmhouse, nor homestead, nor blue smoke curling above thatched roofs, half hidden by orchards of apple trees, do you once behold along its track. A sort of solitude is ever there; not the grand old solitude of Nature's making, but her milder daughter, that other solitude which meekly bears the traces of man's yoke.

Along that road a peasant lad of twelve years old or so, was walking on a hot summer's day some years back. He had curly fair hair, a fresh and merry face, bright as a sunbeam, a quick look, and a frank happy smile. He was very cleanly though very poorly dressed, but he wore his blue blouse, faded by many a washing, with as jaunty an air as if it had been a prince's garment. His little cloth cap was set on one side on his head, and gave him quite a saucy look, and he stepped along the hot sunny road as lightly as though this burning summer's noon were fanned by the freshest breezes of early spring.

Suddenly he stood still. From a field of corn on his right hand rose a girlish voice singing the old and beautiful Advent hymn, "Adeste Fideles," in tones so sweet and clear that the boy listened like one entranced, whilst the voice went on pouring forth its sweet music, filling that summer landscape with the joyful praises of the Lord.

"I must see who it is," thought the lad. "I did not know there was such a bird as that in all Manneville." He lightly leaped across the ditch which divided the road from the cornfield, then creeping along the tall wheat, he stole softly in the direction of the voice till he could see its owner. He saw a very small girl about his own age as he thought, whom he re-cognized at once as the daughter of a weaver, whose tumble-down old house stood not far from his mother's cottage. She was sitting in the grass outside the cornfield, and the long stick ending in a bunch of fluttering rags which she held in her right hand, told the lad her occu-pation. She was too small and too weak for other labour, so she sat there the whole day long to keep away from the ripening corn bold and hungry little spar-rows, or such foraging hens as might stray from distant farmyards in search of booty. She was a very little creature, very demure and grave, with a small pale face, wistful dark eyes, and very dark hair. She wore a little close-fitting black cap, according to the fashion of the country, and it added to the weird-like look of her little wan face. Her other garments were plain and poor enough indeed, but as the boy knew from previous observation, strangely neat and precise in their cut and fashion. She now sat with her head so turned that she could not see the lad, who crouched low in the grass, and kept as quiet as he well could in order not to startle her. He hoped, indeed, that she would finish the hymn without detecting him, but a daring cock made his appearance in the pasture field, deliberately he strutted towards the corn. The girl waved her stick, and at once perceived the boy's head and staring eyes peeping up above the grass. In vain he dived down; it was too late; she ceased singing that very moment. The boy, feeling discovered, sat up, and there was a pause, during which the pair looked at each other very gravely.

"I wish you would go on," at length said the lad.

To this request the little girl gave no sort of answer, but continued looking at him with the immoveable countenance of a young sphinx.

" I wish you had not seen me," he resumed, after waiting in vain for a reply. " You have a beautiful voice; oh! so beautiful!"

The little girl shook her rod at a chattering flock of sparrows, but remained mute.

" I know you," he continued, nothing daunted, " we live close to each other, but I never hear you sing. Indeed, I never hear you talk at all. I said to my mother the other day : ' The weaver's little girl is dumb.' "

On hearing this, the young songstress smiled, and showed the lad two rows of pretty little white teeth.

" Do go on," he entreated. " I shall look another way if you like; but oh, do go on."

His looks and tones expressed so great a longing to hear her, that the little maiden relented, and without saying a word again, broke forth into song. She finished the " Adeste Fideles," and, un- asked, she began another hymn. This she sang through, still in the same clear beautiful voice, which would have made any music enchanting, but which, when giving utterance to the grand old tunes that have been for ages on the lips of wor- shipping generations, sent the boy to the the seventh heaven. His laughing lips quivered with emotion, and his saucy eyes grew so dim that the blue sky, the yellow corn, and the little singer herself all vanished from his sight in a mist. But this was soon over. The little girl got tired of singing, and the boy, stepping through the grass, coolly sat down by her side, and opened a conversation, in which information leading to questioning played a prominent part.

" My name is Louis Picard. What is yours ? Rénée Deschamps. I like Rénée. And so you have lost your mother. My father is dead, too. He was a tailor.

Yours is a weaver, I know; I have seen him at his loom. My mother is a dress-maker. We are from Fontaine, you know. We came to Manneville six months ago, because rent is cheaper here. I am to be a tailor, my mother says. I hate it. You would not like to be a tailor, would you? Of course not. What are you to be? Nothing. You are too weak. Why, how old are you?"

"Sixteen," answered Rénée.

On hearing this reply Louis started. Could this little creature so pale, so thin, really be four years his elder? He looked into her face, and he saw that there was no childishness in it. A grave young face it was, rather sad, indeed, and there was something womanly, too, about the little slender figure—that tiny frame in which dwelt the clear beautiful voice.

"Why do I never hear you sing at home?" suddenly asked Louis.

"I never sing unless when I am out and alone," answered the girl. "My father does not like to hear me."

Youth is quick in jumping at conclusions. The weaver's saturnine countenance, Rénée's sad looks, a sound of subdued weeping which he had heard one evening from their house, helped to build up a little story, unhappily not wide from the truth, of which Rénée was the poor ill-used heroine. He looked at her with sad wonder. That dainty young bird, whose song was so sweet in his ears, found no favour in the eyes of its owner, and could not even warble its song in its rude cage! Louis made no comment, but shook his head over Rénée's hard lot, then talked of other things.

" You know the old schoolmaster," he remarked, with a kindling look: " well, he has got a piano and I am to see it. Perhaps he will let you see it also." This half promise Rénée received with much calmness, yet Louis pursued with unabated enthusiasm. " Then there is the church organ, which is so old that no one can play on it now."

" My mother heard it," interrupted Rénée.

" Did she ! well."

Louis looked breathless, but Rénée, shaking her head demurely, implied unutterable things.

" Oh! *I* have heard the organ in Fontaine," said Louis, " but still I shall like to see this one, and the schoolmaster is to take me up to the gallery; perhaps he will take you, too."

This time Rénée looked interested. And so Louis talked and Rénée listened, and she sang again, and the hours went on, and Louis, who was going to Fontaine, on an errand for his mother, and who was to come back to Manneville as quickly as his feet could carry him, spent the best part of that summer day with Rénée, and when they parted the two friends agreed to meet the next day.

The church of Manneville was very old, and bore tokens of those remote days when Manneville—now a poor Norman village—played its part in feudal story. Its stained glass windows sent many a glorious tint of purple and azure on the mutilated effigies of knights and abbots, resting in calm sleep on their stone beds, and though its lofty organ was mute now, and never pealed forth the solemn "Te Deum," or the joyful "Gloria," its rich brown oak and many tall tubes bore witness to the munificent piety which raised it more than two hundred years ago. Manneville had been very proud of its organ once. It had gloried in its grand music; it had boasted of it when Fontaine and other towns and villages scarcely knew what an organ was; and now that ruthless Time had silenced this old friend, Manneville, ´ though it could boast no more, was tenacious of that past glory. That the organ of Manneville had been the best of organs, that its voice had been the most powerful and yet the sweetest and clearest which ever organ had, was a settled article of belief with every son and daughter of Manneville, but with none more so than with the old schoolmaster, who, on a sunny summer evening, a week after the meeting of Louis and Rénée,

took them both up the dark stone staircase in order to show them the inner
mechanism of the instrument. Rénée
was too much awestruck to utter a word,
but Louis was all ardour and curiosity,
and the old man, who had been the last
organist in Manneville, answered him very
willingly. His head was white as snow,
his face was covered with wrinkles, his
body was bent, his step was unsteady;
but between him and the boy of twelve
there was the strong link of a common
passion—music.

"Oh! how fine it must have been,"
said Louis, with a sigh of regret, "how
very fine!"

"Fine!" echoed the old schoolmaster,
in his thin quavering voice. "I should
think so! You never heard anything like
it—never! Do not tell me of the organ
of Fontaine," he added, testily, "I have
heard it, and I say it was nothing to ours,
and for twenty years and more I played
upon it, and this was an organ indeed,
and those were times for Manneville."

He half closed his eyes, and let the past come back to him in its dim glories of music, and tapers, and incense. Yes, those were times for Manneville, when its organ could still speak, and its organist was not the lonely, widowed, and white-haired schoolmaster, but a man, happy, young, and strong, with a pretty rosy wife and two laughing children—all three now sleeping soundly in the green church-yard of Manneville.

Rénée too, thought of the past, and peeping down into the empty church below, she wished she could have heard that wonderful creature, the organ, of which her mother had so often told her, and which Louis raved about. Then, childlike, she wandered from this thought to other thoughts. A little bird had flown into the church, and now hopping from bench to bench with a gravity of bearing which amused Rénée. She watched it till it flew away through the broken pane of a remote window; then she looked down once more. The quiet church was now full of sunshine, streaming in through the open door, pouring its red gold on the broken stone floor, and creeping up to the altar steps as if it, too, wished to worship and fling its gorgeous radiance there in silent adoration.

Louis, more practical, was wondering, in the meanwhile, whether that dead part would know no second birth.

" And can the organ never be played upon again?" he asked.

" Oh, yes, by all means," replied the schoolmaster, with cutting sarcasm, " when Manneville has three thousand francs to spend upon it !"

Rénée clasped her hands on hearing the enormous sum mentioned, but Louis, nothing daunted, said again—

" Could not you play if I were to attempt to blow the bellows ?"

The schoolmaster's lip quivered as he said: " The Sunday after my last child was buried, the organ went wrong. I have never played on it since then, and I never shall. Come down, children."

" If you please," persisted Louis, " I should like so to hear Rénée's voice in the church. May she sing ?"

The schoolmaster, who had heard the boy talk of Rénée's wonderful voice, and who felt some curiosity to hear her, gave the required permission, and Rénée, after a little coaxing from Louis, was persuaded to sing that most musical of anthems, the " Salve Regina." Every one knows how much finer even a fine voice sounds when it is heard under the arched roof of a church. Rénée's voice now sent Louis into an ecstacy, and even the old schoolmaster was moved to the very heart by the sweet, clear notes which the little maiden poured forth. But scarcely had she got half way through the anthem when she ceased abruptly, and, with a pale scared face, looked at a stern middle-aged man, who stood in the gloomy doorway of the staircase. He beckoned to her silently, and then, trembling with fear, Rénée followed him out without saying a word.

M 2

"That is Rénée's father!" exclaimed Louis, full of dismay; "how unlucky that he should have come back so early from Fontaine! Do you think he will beat Rénée, sir?"

The schoolmaster shook his head. The weaver had the name of being a very hard man, and it was much to be feared that Rénée would not escape scatheless. Louis was to take his first lesson in music on the schoolmaster's old cracked piano that night; but for all that his heart felt like lead within his breast, as he thought of Rénée's trouble.

Madame Picard was sitting alone that evening, thinking how hard it was to get dresses to make in a poor place like Manneville, and what a trouble it was to be the mother of a boy who would learn music— what for, good heavens?—and who hated being a tailor, when her cottage door opened and in walked her neighbour, the weaver.

Jean Deschamps was a man of few words. Civility was not his amiable weakness. Sharply and curtly he delivered his errand, standing near the door all the time. Madame Picard's Louis and his Rénée had been holding private meetings in the fields, in the church even, everywhere, in short, and he, Rénée's father, forbade it now, once for all.

On coming to settle in Manneville, Madame Picard had resolved to agree with every man, woman, and child in it, and to endorse every possible statement, opinion, and theory she might hear broached. She now turned up her eyes in horror, at the tale the weaver delivered, and clasping her hands thanked her neighbour; but would he not sit down?—she could not realize it yet. Perhaps he would explain? Jean Deschamps came for war, and he found peace. He came prepared to drive his enemy into the last corner of maternal love, and she held up such a white flag of truce that he must needs hold a parley. He took the proffered chair, and condescended to explain.

" You see, Madame Picard," he said,

"I do not want Rénée to sing. The creature is weak enough and good for little, but if she sings, all her strength will go out in her voice, and she will be good for nothing. Besides, I hate singing, music, and all those noises."

Madame Picard looked admiringly at the weaver. That was the way to rear a child, of course it was! Oh! if he would only tell her, a poor widowed woman, how to manage her unruly boy! Jean Deschamps gazed kindly at the widow. He thought her a sensible woman, that he did; and, having heard her case, he advised a good caning as the surest means of giving Louis a proper liking for a tailor's craft, and especially as the best cure of that mania for music—a sin second only to Rénée's singing. Madame Picard received this humane suggestion with an admiring gratitude, which convinced the weaver that she was not merely a wise woman, but the wisest of women. As he left her that evening, after partaking of a drop of brandy with her, and went back to the house where Rénée was crying herself to sleep, Jean Deschamps had already conceived a project, which became known to Manneville a fortnight later, when the banns of his marriage with Madame Picard were read from the pulpit. And thus it came to pass, that Louis and Rénée, who had been forbidden to meet, now lived in the same house; that Rénée learned dress-making with her step-mother, and that Louis became a weaver under his step-father's tuition; but that singing and music were more prohibited than ever.

The opportunities for disobedience were, unfortunately, very few. Louis was kept so close to the loom that there was no getting at the schoolmaster's piano, and it was only now and then on a Sunday afternoon that Rénée and he could go out together.

Side by side, the two children, for Rénée was little more than a child, wandered out into the country till they reached some shady cavée or some lonely field, where only the birds in the tree could hear them. Then they both sat down, and Rénée would sing to her friend, charming his heart away with the heavenly music of her fresh young voice. These were divine moments for the boy. As he lay in the grass looking at the sky, as he saw the tender and golden green of the sunlit trees quivering on that background of soft azure, and listened to Rénée, his very soul seemed to float away with the little white clouds that sailed across those fields of blue air. Sometimes, conquered by the passion of melody, he would fling himself on his face and hide the tears of delight which he could not check; but oftener than all, for Louis though impassioned was also strong, he would close his eyes, shut out even the fair aspects of Nature, and give himself up calmly to a born musician's most perfect happiness. For though no one knew it, not even Louis himself, a great gift slept within the peasant boy's breast. There are " many mansions" in Art as well as in Heaven. Some are as kings or creators in the world of

sweet sounds, calling them forth and
giving them life; others are only worshippers, who listen and admire, and even of
these "Many are called, and few are
chosen." It is a rare gift to feel the
beauty of anything in its fulness, and a
rarer still is it to love that thing with all
the passion of a human heart. Even
Rénée, though she had a correct ear, had
not so keen or perfect an appreciation of
her own singing as Louis who only listened
to her. She sang as any little bird might
sing : happily and carelessly.

When she was tired, her society was
none the less acceptable to Louis ; for she
became as mute as a mouse, and listened
to his dreams of the future as he planned
them out for her benefit. "When I am
a man I shall do as I like, of course,"
Louis would say, "and then I shall take
lessons from the old schoolmaster and
learn music on his pianoforte; then I
shall write to the Minister, or to the
Emperor, or some one, and get the money
to put the organ of Manneville to rights ;

then I shall become the organist. Eh! Rénée." And little Rénée would nod and smile. But the very first of these " thens " never came to pass ; for the schoolmaster died, and his poor old cracked piano was sold to a lady in Fontaine, and with his own eyes Louis saw it taken away in a cart.

" No more jingling, now," sarcastically said the weaver.

Louis felt the taunt as it was intended he should feel it—in his very heart. He was about sixteen when this misfortune occurred, and whether because the blow was so great that he required consolation, or because he was tall, strong, and as manly-looking as if he had been twenty, Louis suddenly took it into his head to make love to Rénée, who was as little, as slight, and almost as pale as ever.

It was on a Sunday afternoon, whilst the weaver was safe at the café, and the pair, who had stolen out into the fields, were sitting side by side in the shadow of a green hedge, that Louis, to whom Rénée had been singing with her heavenly voice, remarked, coolly :

"When you are my wife, Rénée——"

"What !" cried Rénée, with a start.

"Well, do you want to marry anyone else, now ?" he asked sharply.

"That is not it, Louis ; but think how much older I am than you are."

"Are you bigger, and stronger, and taller, too ? Come, Rénée, you would not go and marry anyone else, when you know all I have borne for your sake. Why, I should have run away long ago if it were not for you."

Rénée knew that, and felt silenced. Besides, she was a meek little thing, and always did Louis' bidding. Moreover, she knew how he doated on her voice. How could she give that voice to another ? So she made no further objection when Louis pursued :

"When you are my wife, and I am organist of Manneville, we shall have a house of our own of course, and I shall have a piano, and you shall sing——"

"A pretty tune I shall make you both sing to, you young scapegraces!" cried a wrathful voice behind the hedge, above which the weaver's head soon appeared. How he had seen them and stolen after them, Louis could not imagine, but there he was, forbidding the banns. He would have done more if he had dared, but Louis was too strong and sturdy now to be struck, and what was more, he looked as if it might be dangerous to lay a finger on Rénée in his presence. So the weaver keeping safe behind the hedge, ordered Rénée home forthwith, and when she had obeyed silently, he turned to Louis, and said sarcastically :

"You cannot marry Rénée without your mother's consent till you are twenty-five—a long time to wait, Louis: nine years. You can learn how to play on the organ in the meanwhile." And chuckling to himself, he walked away.

"Learn how to play on the organ ? ay, and that I will," muttered Louis between his set teeth, "and sooner than you think, too."

For the sake of his mother, who lived in wholesome dread of her stern husband, Louis had been a tolerably dutiful step-son, but he now felt roused to revolt, and the very next week war began. During that week, Louis and Rénée had been lectured and scolded daily. The nine years which French law exacted from Louis before he could marry Rénée without the consent of his mother, and in reality of his step-father, for the poor woman had no will of her own, seemed all too brief to that bitter-minded old gentleman. He hated his step-son, and if he did not turn him out of the house forthwith, it was for the sake of his earnings at the loom; so he made up in worrying, what he could not take out of Louis in more substantial ill-usage. But at the end of a week, the weaver made a discovery which filled him with the direst wrath. He bided his opportunity, and one night as the church clock of Manneville was striking twelve, he went up to his daughter's room, entered it abruptly, and found Rénée sitting up by her window, and looking out on the moonlit road, above which chill autumn mists were floating.

" Why are you up and dressed at this hour ?" he asked, sternly.

Rénée could not answer—her fear was so great when she saw her father standing before her, with the flickering light of a tallow candle shining on his harsh face.

" And where is Louis ?" he continued. " Out; gone to Fontaine to take lessons from the organist, and you sit up to let him in, do you ! Well, you need not. I shall let him in to-night, and settle accounts with *you* Rénée, to-morrow."

He vanished, locking the door outside, and leaving Rénée half dead with fear, not for herself, but for Louis. Suddenly a bright thought struck her. She climbed up on a chest of drawers, opened a little casement above it, crept out through it, and lightly jumped down on a landing. Then she stole downstairs to the garden, and whilst her father was watching at the front door, she crept out through a gap in the hedge into the open country. She was soon on the high road, walking towards Fontaine in order to meet and warn Louis.

Never before in all her life had Rénée been out so late, and being but a timid little thing, she felt very much afraid. It was all so lonely, so silent, and so solemn in the pale moonlight. Then it felt so chill, too, and those white mists which hung above the fields, made Rénée's blood flow more slowly in her veins, and seem to freeze the very marrow in her bones. She walked up and down to keep herself warm, then, feeling tired, she sat down on the lowest step of a wayside cross, and waited there in vain; the moon waned, the sky broke with the grayness of early dawn, and Louis came not. They had missed each other! Whilst Rénée was stealing out of the garden, Louis had come home along the road, but not receiving her usual signal, he had, instead of coming to the house, stolen into a neighbouring shed, where he was now fast asleep on a bundle of straw.

Poor Rénée, who had not the comfort of knowing this much, stole home. Cold and heartsick, she got back to her room without having been missed; but hers was the severest cost of that night's work, for when her father came to unlock her room the next morning, he found Rénée lying on her bed in a burning fever, unable to move or to speak.

Rénée lay for a month between life and death, and when she recovered, her beautiful voice was gone. Louis was the first whom she told of this, and she added, as a matter of course:

"And I think, Louis, that as my voice is gone, you had better tell my father that you give me up, and perhaps he will let you learn music in peace."

"And so you thought it was for your voice that I liked you?" cried Louis, in hot indignation.

Yes, Rénée had thought that; and seeing that she was loved for her own sake, she felt too happy for one moment, but the next she could not help saying:

"Oh! Louis! how shall we manage?"

Death settled that question : for soon
after Rénée's recovery the mother of Louis
died. At once the youth's resolve was
taken. He would go away; go and try
his fortunes, and come back and be
organist of Manneville, and marry Rénée
if she would only wait for him. Rénée
raised her soft dark eyes to his.

"I shall wait for you till I die," she
said.

The weaver would have tried to keep
Louis, just to vex and thwart him, if the
young man had not gone away without
saying a word to any one, save Rénée.
He vanished from the house one morning,
and after a while Rénée felt as if he had
vanished out of her life. No one knew
whither he was gone, no one knew what
he was doing, no one had seen or met
Louis, or heard of him, till two years
after his departure, a report reached
Manneville, that Louis Picard had died in
one of the Paris hospitals. It was the
weaver who told Rénée, and with a low

chuckling laugh. She heard, but did not believe him. When we love and are young, the being we love wears a charm against all harm. Death, which can lay whole kingdoms waste, and level nations in the grave has no power over the beloved one of a young heart.

" It is not true, it cannot be true; Louis is not dead," Renée said to herself, not merely on that day, but on every day that followed it for weeks and months; but as time passed and brought no tidings from the absent one, Renée sank into that dull apathy which is twin sister to despair. Louis had been gone four years, when his enemy, the weaver, was found dead in his bed one morning, by his poor little daughter. It was a cruel shock, and the sorrow it inflicted was not lessened by a discovery Renée made after the funeral. In looking over her father's possessions, she found the fragment of a letter addressed to herself by Louis, but what the purport of the letter had been, and whether it had been written before or

after the report of his death, there
was nothing to show. All Rénée's
wounds bled afresh as she held the
mutilated letter in her hand. Was Louis
living or dead, had he forgotten her, or
would he come back some day? Who
could tell! not Rénée surely, only one
thing she knew.

"I will wait for him till I die," she
said to her own heart, as she put the
letter away. It is the lot of many
women to wait so; and Rénée, meek
and trusting, bore her fate with silent
patience. She never spoke of the hope
that lived within her. She never complained that her youth was wasting away
in this lonely vigil for one who seemed
to have forgotten her; she never even
uttered his name, but she lived alone in
her father's old tumbledown house, tenderly keeping the memory of the past in
her faithful heart. And thus her life was
passing slowly and heavily, when there
occurred an unexpected event to break its
monotony. Rénée was coming home one

evening from her day's work, for Manneville
is faithful to the old custom of having its
dresses made at home, when she found
with much surprise, a strange woman
sitting on the threshold of her dwelling,
and evidently waiting for her.

" Are you Rénée Deschamps ?" asked
the stranger, who was middle-aged, sharp-
tongued, and sharp-eyed.

" That is my name," answered Rénée.

" Well you are little," said the stranger,
emphatically; " open the door will you.
I am tired of waiting here."

Rénée did as she was bid. She felt
perplexed and amazed, and a wild hope
fluttered at her breast. Was this imperative stranger bringing tidings of her
long-lost Louis? But no, her visitor soon
dispelled the illusion.

" I am your Aunt Marie," she said,
sitting down at once. " I quarrelled with
your father on your poor mother's wedding-day, and we never made it up. Well
he is dead now, poor fellow. Hearing
you were alone, I came to see you, or

rather," she added, casting the contemptuous look of a town woman on Rénée's bare country home, " to take you away with me to Rouen, where I live, as you know."

Rénée was startled, frightened, and yet pleased. Perhaps she might hear something of Louis in Rouen! So she accepted her aunt's proposal, and went away with her the next morning.

Madame Reux was a childless widow. She had a little income on which she could keep a servant that was willing to work and expect no wages. Such a party she hoped to secure in Rénée, who, being meek and humble, and having never had a will of her own, yielded to her aunt's wishes without demur. Yet even Rénée soon found that she had exchanged freedom for servitude, a home for a prison. Madame Reux lived in a dark and dingy lane, in a dismal old house where Rénée felt smothered for want of air. Madame Reux said that the twilight which reigned in her home was the best thing in the

world for weak eyes, and rejoiced over
the absence of bright sun and blue sky.
Both were interrupted by a dead wall
facing her windows. This was the back
of a convent, which was, however, poor
Rénée's only comfort, for on a Sunday
morning the full tones of an organ rose
from its little chapel, filling Rénée's heart
with mingled sorrow and delight. The
sounds of that organ, the first which she
had ever heard, were Rénée's only link
with that past of which she had hoped to
find some token in Rouen. No one knew
anything about Louis Picard in that large
city, no one had ever heard of the peasant
boy who was to become the organist of
Manneville.

Rénée was pining away like a bird in
her cage, when her aunt luckily got tired
of seeing her little pale face and sad eyes.

"Go back to Manneville, my dear," she
said to her, at the end of six months.
"You have bad health, and the money I
have spent on your journey here has been
wasted; but you have seen Rouen and

enjoyed yourself, and I don't grudge it."

Rénée might have replied that she had seen the dead wall of the convent and heard its organ, but she was a meek little soul, and took her aunt's generosity as granted.

The autumn day was cold and still when Rénée alighted from the diligence in Fontaine, and prepared to walk on alone to Manneville. The road was bleak and very lonely, but Rénée's heart felt lighter than it had felt for many a day. Only once it sank within her. She was passing by the field where Louis had found her scaring the birds away from the corn, and heard her singing the "Adeste Fideles." Brown and bare was that field now. No yellow corn was ripening in the summer sun. No little pilfering birds had to be frightened away; no humming-bee was rifling the wild thyme in the pasture field; no happy singing Rénée, no delighted listening Louis were there now; far as she looked, Rénée only saw the naked furrowed earth stretching away before

her. Thus too, was her life—her life so
young still, but from which brightness,
pleasure, and song had departed. So
Renée thought, forgetting that the seed
of another harvest was ripening beneath
that brown earth, and that thus, too, it
might yet be with her.

The grayness of twilight was settling
on Manneville as Renée approached it.
She saw the old church on the hill, and
little lights twinkling here and there
around it; but though Renée looked wistfully at the village, she shunned its steep
main street, and took a quiet lane which
led her to her own house in the fields.
She met no one on her way, and when she
entered the dwelling in which her youth
had been spent, when she struck a light
and kindled a little crackling fire of rape
stalks, and sat down looking at it, Renée,
though at home once more, felt that sense
of loneliness upon her which comes to us
when we have left the dead behind us,
and must needs journey on through life
without them.

Still, Renée was young, and to youth

many things are pleasant. The sun shone
so brightly the next day, the sky was so
clear and blue, that Rénée felt cheerful as
she looked into the fields—all white with
the night's frost. This was Sunday, too,
and when the familiar Manneville bells
came pealing on the air, Rénée's heart
had a throb of gladness. She liked that
old church dearly, and had never found in
all Rouen one that she liked half so well.
Neither Notre Dame nor Saint Ouen could
make Rénée forget her early love.

" Thank God to be at home once
more !" she said to her own heart, as
she took her seat on the old bench where
she had sat since she could remember. It
was early, and the church was empty still,
but Rénée liked that. She wanted to pray
quietly, and collect her thoughts before
the congregation came in. She was kneeling, and had closed her eyes, feeling,
perhaps, that she could not well help
being a little distracted at seeing all the
well-known faces around her, when mass
began. It began, and with it there pealed

through the church, clear, deep, and strong, the voice of the long silent organ.

If Rénée did not start up and utter a cry, it was because the very excess of her surprise kept her motionless and mute. But she shook from head to foot, and felt in a trance of amazed delight. If the test of music be in its power over a human heart, never surely was there music out of heaven like that to which Rénée listened then. She hid her face in her hands and let happy, grateful tears, flow through her little fingers. In the meanwhile, the organ poured forth its glorious tide of sound, now triumphant, now pathetic, now solemn and tender; and, what with the music and the delight of knowing that Louis had come back, for she did not doubt it one moment, Rénée felt that perfect bliss which life grants to few, and to those few but rarely.

And now mass was over, the organ was hushed, and the congregation poured out. Rénée shyly lingered as long as she could, till the church was well nigh empty, then she rose and slowly walked out. The ordeal she had wished to delay was waiting for her beneath the church porch, for she reached it at the same time with Louis, who had just left the vestry, and was still flushed with the joy and pride of his triumph. All the little world of Manneville was gathered ou the Place outside, and stood there looking on at the meeting of the two lovers.

Louis went up to Rénée and gave her his arm, without uttering a word, and Rénée took it as he gave it, silently, and thus, arm-in-arm, feeling as if they trod on air, now that life had fulfilled its sweetest promises for them, these two happy ones went down the main street of Manneville, hearing their own story told by every looker-on.

" He went to Paris."

" He got the money to repair the organ."

" All these years she waited for him."

" To think of all he went through to learn music. He a weaver, too."

" Her father burned the letters."

" He is our organist now."

" I always liked Rénée."

" God bless them both."

And so the chorus went on till it died away behind Louis and Rénée as they wandered together in the quiet autumn landscape.

" And what have you to tell me, Rénée ?" asked Louis, when his story was ended—a wonderful story of untiring energy—long struggles, and final victory. " What have you been doing all these years ?"

" Waiting for you," tenderly answered Rénée. When, raising her soft dark eyes to his, with a smile, she began to sing very sweetly. For Providence had been kind to the faithful girl who sat and waited, as well as to the brave man who went forth to strive, and Rénée's voice, her beautiful voice, had all come back.

The happiness of Louis would have been perfect if he could have played on the organ of Manneville on his own wedding-day, but as that was impossible, the organist of Fontaine had to come and render him that good service.

Charlotte Morel.

IT is the way of the world to speak of the Middle Ages as if they were dead and buried. It is also the way of the world to rear ponderous books over them, like so many grave-stones—volumes in the pages of which are inscribed epitaphs that are not always records of mediæval virtues.

Dead in most places the Middle Ages are—dead and forgotten. They have left no traces in the lives of men and women; they may linger in a few old churches, or castle walls, or ivied towers, but from the

human mind and heart they have utterly
passed away.

But far from the tracks of the railway,
travellers now and then find out spots
where mediæval life is not dead, but sleeping. The men wear coats, and the women
chignons; but beneath these outward
signs of the nineteenth century lie modes
of thought and habits of life which certainly belong to another age than this.
These places are mostly found abroad;
little mousey provincial towns are they,
not sufficiently interesting to attract anti-
quarians, and too poor to stimulate enter-
prise; places in which life is as dull and
as torpid as it was three hundred years
ago, and more.

To this quiet tribe belongs Verrières, in
one of the central provinces of France.
Wars and revolutions seem to have passed
over it in vain. It has heard the mighty
whirlwind of a people's wrath, and echoed
to the cannon's roar; but like the enchanted Durandarte, whom Don Quixote
saw in the cave of Montesimos, it has

turned on its side, and taken a philosophical nap.

Money is of great account in places like this, and money has reached its full value in Verrières. The little humdrum town, with its long, silent street, and its green gardens spreading behind its old houses so quaint and grey, thinks a great deal of Mammon, not as seen in Three per Cents., or in railway shares, or even in banknotes; but Mammon as he shows himself to his worshippers in gold, silver, or copper aspect, or in such goods as are daily exchanged for the same.

Thanks to Mammon, therefore, Monsieur Morel, the richest man in Verrières, held a high position in his native place. Monsieur Morel was a grocer and general dealer. He literally fed and clothed Verrières. Monsieur Morel sold flour, bacon, eggs, sugar, colonial goods, spirits and wine even, crockery, hardware, boots and shoes, cloths, silks, calico, linen, and every species of cheap stuff, not liable to sudden changes of fashion. He not only fed and clothed Verrières, as we said, but a whole set of villages and hamlets which clustered around it as well; and as no competitor had ever stepped in to make him lower his prices, which were rather high, Monsieur Morel soon became a rich man, and grew richer with every year. He lived in a very old house, with many windows to it; windows high and narrow which, as well as the steep roof and massive chimney-stacks, spoke of a bygone age. In the broad and lofty rooms of that house—and it had many—he stored away his multifarious goods. Casks of butter, bales of coffee, sacks full of flour, piles of sugar-loaves in blue paper, could be seen by the admiring eyes of the children of Verrières, through the dusty and grated windows of the ground-floor. But still greater wonders were reported of the first, second, and third floors of Monsieur Morel's house. Piles upon piles of shining silks and fine broad-cloths were there, it was said; precious goods, never visited in their solemn and dusky retreat save by

Monsieur Morel and his clerk Lenoir, a
little, wiry old man, who went through
life with a pen behind his ear. These two,
Monsieur Morel and Lenoir, assisted by
two stout servant-women, attended to the
shop. This was not in the street, as
might have been expected, but in the yard
at the back of the house. A low, dingy-
looking shop it was, in which perpetual
twilight reigned, and where the sun never
entered, but a shop in which the chink of
money was heard all the day long, and all
the year round. Light and sun it had had
in its early days, when the yard merged
into a pleasant garden, bounded by a little
river which flowed between willows and
aspen trees. But when Monsieur Morel's
business so increased that he knew not
where to turn for spare room, the garden
was sacrificed. Outhouses were raised in
its stead, and a skylight roof extending
from them to the large old house in front,
enclosed the whole yard; in which, thanks
to this shelter, more goods were stowed
away.

Madame Morel was young when this was done, and she sorely lamented the loss of the garden where she used to sit on summer evenings, knitting and looking at the flowing river and the aspen trees and hoary willows, with the flushed sunset sky above them. To reconcile her to the change, her husband turned the yard into a sort of green-house. Glossy ivy was trained against the walls, and soon covered them with sombre verdure. With ivy mingled light summer creepers that climbed up to the skylight, and hung thence over sacks, and bales, and packages in graceful banners, receiving air from a high-arched gateway that led from the street to the shop, and thriving in their captivity.

Very cool, green, and pleasant looked this yard from the street. Strangers wondered at it, and the people of Verrières were proud of it. Madame Morel did not live to enjoy it. She died when her first child was born. Her widowed husband never married again ; but though caring little for them himself, he cherished and tended the ivy and the creepers for his dead wife's sake.

Sovereigns have their cares. Wars, foreign alliances, bickerings with royal brothers and sisters, embitter the lives of ladies and gentlemen who wear crowns and sit on thrones. No wonder, therefore, that, apart from his wife's death, Monsieur Morel had troubles incidental to his position. The chief of these was, that the late Madame Morel had not given him a son, but a daughter.

"Ah, Lenoir," he would say to his clerk, "the mother-abbess gives me the best account of the little thing's temper and abilities; my own eyes tell me that she is both pretty and healthy. But it is a great trial that I have not got a Charles, but a Charlotte. The business, you know."

"It is a great pity that Mademoiselle Charlotte is not Monsieur Charles," Lenoir would ruefully answer. "It certainly was a great mistake." And this error of the

late Madame Morel became a standing
grievance between these two.

When Madame Morel's mistake was
about seven years old, she came home to
her father's on a week's holiday. A very
pretty, quiet, demure child, with black
eyes and a rosy face, was Charlotte Morel.
And very pretty she looked when she acted
as bridesmaid to her father's sister, who
married Monsieur Roussel, the notary,
about this time. Monsieur Roussel was a
widower, and his son, Henri, a lad of
twelve, took a great fancy to Mademoiselle Charlotte. He sat by her at the
wedding dinner; he danced with her in
the evening; and when she complained of
being fatigued, he chivalrously put her on
his back, and carried her home. Monsieur Morel, who was already looking out
for a son-in-law, and who liked the aspect
of this handsome and spirited lad, slapped
him on the back, and said, cheeringly:

"That's right, Henri; carry your little
wife."

Upon which, Henri, turning his frank

face and blue eyes to Charlotte, said, gaily :

" Will you marry me, Charlotte ? Eh, will you marry me ?"

The proposal, coming as it did when Charlotte was on her suitor's back, with her arms around his neck, was an awkward one. She looked shy and doubtful; before she could answer, Henri's uncle and godfather, Monsieur Roussel, the farmer, interfered, and said, sarcastically :

" Do not say yes, Charlotte, or you will repent it, for you see Henri has a temper."

Henri became crimson, and bit his lip.

" Henri will improve," hesitatingly said his father.

" Please to put me down ?" asked Charlotte.

" I will not," passionately replied the boy. " I will carry you, whether you like it or not, mamzelle."

Charlotte submitted; but when they reached home, and Henri put her down, she would neither look at him nor bid him good-night.

" You are a sulky little thing," he said, angrily.

A remark which Charlotte did not deign to answer.

The breach might have widened if Mademoiselle Morel had not gone back to her convent the very next morning. When these two met again, she had grown to be a decorous young lady, and he a civil young man; and neither attempted to renew the passages of their childhood.

Charlotte was about eighteen when Monsieur Morel said one morning to Lenoir : " I must see about a son-in-law."

But where was the young man to be found who could be both Charlotte Morel's husband and Monsieur Morel's successor? Where was the lover and the man of business? All Verrières could not yield him. The shrewd, sharp man was either married, or too old, or blind of an eye, and the agreeable man was either a spendthrift, or a bad accountant, or simply empty-headed.

"I must try Henri Roussel," said Monsieur Morel, with a sigh. Monsieur Lenoir heard, and groaned, and turned up his eyes. Matters must be bad. indeed for Monsieur Morel to take such a resolve as this.

Henri Roussel was now a very fine, manly-looking young fellow, with plenty of brains, but with a reckless, ungovernable temper, which had already led him into various scrapes, and which kept his father, a weak, nervous man, and his step-mother, a timid, yielding woman, in a constant state of fever and uneasiness. Monsieur Roussel was the notary of Verrières, and he lived in the house next to that of his brother-in-law, another gray old mansion, but with two gilt 'scutcheons over the gateway, and numerous blue, red, and yellow bills, announcing sales of farms, and châteaux, and fields, and vineyards, stuck on either side of the entrance. To him Monsieur Morel first broached his proposal.

"Please yourself; but neither you nor

anyone else will do any good with Henri," despondently answered Monsieur Roussel. "In this very room I told him so only yesterday."

The room which had witnessed this paternal denunciation was a square and lofty apartment. It had a dingy bookcase full of ponderous law-books, a dingy table covered with yellow papers, and a dull, rusty-looking iron safe, no doubt full of title-deeds and valuable documents. It was not a fascinating room for a lively young man.

"Perhaps he will like business better than the law," said Monsieur Morel.

His brother-in-law shook his head.

"Henri can live on the little fortune his mother left him," he said, "and Henri will like nothing. Mind," he added, expanding his hands, "you take him on your own responsibility."

Thus comforted, Monsieur Morel went down stairs. His sister was knitting in a dull parlour, with her two daughters by her. When they had been sent away, and her brother explained his plans, the good lady dropped ten stitches of her knitting.

"Poor Charlotte!" she said. "Why, he will break the child's heart with his temper."

Monsieur Morel said something about some one who was not so black as he was painted, upon which he was told that he did not know Henri Roussel.

"Well, then," he retorted, losing patience, "I cannot help myself; beggars cannot be choosers."

And he went forthwith to find the sinner—whom he had always liked, to say the truth—at the end of the garden. A pleasant, sunlit garden was this—half garden, half orchard, and sloping down to the river-side. Monsieur Morel walked down trim paths, with beds of stocks and wallflowers blossoming very sweetly in the light shade of apple trees, till he came to the river. There he found Henri Roussel in his shirt-sleeves, mending and hammering a boat with right good will. He was twenty-three then, a tall and very handsome young man, with a tinge of red in his yellow locks, but with a frank look in his blue eyes and an open smile, which Monsieur Morel had always liked. At once, in few but plain words, he expounded his errand and made his proposal. Henri heard him, sitting on the side of the boat, with the hammer in one hand and his chin resting on the palm of the other.

" Thank you, uncle," he said gravely; " but you know I never took to the law."

" The law is one thing, and business is another," replied Monsieur Morel.

" Yes; I want life, motion, variety. Business gives these—the law does not. And you want me to marry Charlotte," continued the young man, gravely. " You know I am by no means so rich as she is."

" That is *my* business."

" But how will she like it, uncle ?"

" That is *your* business," answered Monsieur Morel, smiling.

The colour deepened on the young man's cheek ; he was silent awhile, then he made one last objection.

" My father, my step-mother, my two sisters all declare that I have a bad and violent temper. Are you willing,' nevertheless, to trust me with your daughter's happiness ?"

" I am," stoutly replied Monsieur Morel; " for if you have a warm temper, for which the colour of your hair may be answerable, I believe you have also a generous heart, and that you are incapable of making my little Charlotte unhappy."

Henri Roussel said nothing, but his blue eyes were dim and his lips quivered as he rose and held out his hand, which Monsieur Morel grasped cordially. It was a bargain, and the young man came that same evening, not to live in the house, which was not needed, but to have a long business conversation with his uncle. He proved an apt pupil. There was life and activity in the business, as Monsieur Morel had truly said. Henri Roussel had to travel and go about to fairs and markets, and he showed such business talents and gave such satisfaction, that Monsieur

Morel sent for his daughter in order to conclude the matter as soon as possible.

Mademoiselle Charlotte Morel had rarely left her convent, and her few glimpses of the world seemed to have had little effect upon her. She was as quiet and demure as any little nun. Rather little she was, though not ungracefully so—little, but very pretty, with a rosy, round face, charming dimples, lovely black eyes, and glossy black hair. This attractive young person also had an amiable and even temper, and more practical sense than ladies of her years are supposed to possess. Her father laid his plans open to her with perfect candour. His fortune was invested in his business, and his son-in-law must also, if possible, be his successor. He was quite satisfied with Henri Roussel, and though he wished to lay no compulsion upon her, he hoped that his daughter would like the young man. Charlotte heard him out, with her eyes downcast, and her hands folded on her lap, and then said gravely:

" Has he not a bad temper ?"

" Rather hasty, perhaps," reluctantly said Monsieur Morel; " but Henri Roussel would never be to a young and agreeable wife what he may have been to his family, you know."

Charlotte raised her eyebrows in mingled surprise and doubt on hearing this.

" I hope to get old," she said, quaintly.

Monsieur Morel, not knowing what to say, began praising the young man's talent, assiduity, and good looks.

" Henri always begins very well," composedly replied Charlotte, " and I know he is clever."

" And very handsome," persisted Monsieur Morel, shrewdly.

His daughter answered with the untranslateable " comme ça," to which " so-so " is no equivalent; and no more was said on the subject.

To all appearance, matters went on very well between the young people. Charlotte sat and worked in a room next the shop on the ground-floor, and there Henri would go and join her now and then. The door remained open, and from the shop Monsieur Morel watched them with a pleased eye. He saw his pretty daughter sitting near the window, around which the creepers hung. How quiet and demure she looked, with her downcast eyes, whilst Henri Roussel, leaning against the wall, gazed down at her in evident admiration!

" I fancy it will do," thought Monsieur Morel; but to be sure of it, he questioned his daughter. Charlotte was silent awhile; then she said:

" I mistrust him. He had a temper once, and he seems to have lost it."

" Because he is fond of you."

" Ah, but suppose he should cease being fond of me ?"

Now, as ill-luck would have it, Monsieur Morel repeated this conversation to Henri Roussel. The young man heard him, and said nothing, but bit his lip and turned very red. He sometimes rowed Charlotte and his sisters down the river of an evening, and he did so late on the afternoon of this day. The sun was setting behind the old church of Verrières. Blue and gold were in the sky, and mingled in the placid surface of the little stream with the green shadows of the aspens and the willows. The boat floated past quiet gardens; as he rowed, Henri looked at Charlotte with mingled love and anger. The young girl sat still, for Louise, Henri's youngest sister, had fallen asleep on her lap.

"Why do you not trust me, Charlotte?" asked Henri abruptly.

Charlotte raised her eyes in some wonder; then guessing the truth, she coloured a little, but replied, composedly:

"What difference does it make to you whether I trust you or not?"

Her cool tone, her unmoved look, exasperated him. In a moment Henri recovered the temper which the fair Charlotte supposed him to have lost. His eyes flashed, his lips trembled with resentment.

"You must be heartless to put such a question," he said impetuously.

Charlotte looked at him very earnestly:

"Thank you," she said, bowing her head with ironical courtesy. "Pray be so kind as to row me back."

He complied without saying a word. That same evening Charlotte quietly informed her father that she should never marry Henri Roussel.

"The man who cannot rule himself shall never rule me," she said.

Monsieur Morel was much annoyed, and much troubled, he did his best to convince Charlotte that she had better give Henri another trial; but the proposal was evidently so distasteful to her, and she shrank from it with such pain, that he did not insist.

"Very well," he said desperately; "I must send off poor Henri, and you must go back to the convent till I have found some one else."

To this sentence Charlotte submitted without a word. She went away the very next morning. Henri said bitterly:

"I do not know why I regret her: she

did not care a rush for me." And he, too, went, not merely from his uncle's house, but from Verrières, which he left for Paris, and entered a large commercial house.

Nothing came of Monsieur Morel's search for some one else. He lived in hope, and left his daughter safe behind convent walls till she was twenty-one, when grim Death settled his perplexity by calling him very suddenly away one summer morning.

Verrières was much startled by the news, and Verrières' first thought on the subject was a pithy homily on the vanity of human sorrow. Verrières grieved very little for the dead man, but wondered very much who was going to step into his shoes. Several individuals for whose business talents Monsieur Morel had entertained a strong contempt, had visions of purchasing the business, and lording it in the great old house; they sounded Lenoir, the old clerk, and as he heard them out and returned diplomatic replies, they one and all felt pretty sure of success. Monsieur Lenoir was very much perplexed. He consulted with Mademoiselle Morel's nearest relatives, and they all came to the conclusion that Monsieur Roussel, her uncle's brother, ought to be the successful applicant; he was not, indeed, the successor such a man as Monsieur Morel should have had, but he was the least objectionable of all the claimants for the dead man's honours. Monsieur Morel had been dead a fortnight, when Lenoir thought he could broach the subject to his late master's daughter. She had come back for the funeral, and being of age, had no thought of returning to the convent. Her grief was such as a good-hearted girl must feel for the death of a parent of whom she knows little; sincere, but by no means violent. Mademoiselle Charlotte Morel was, in short, in that subdued, but even frame of mind which is perfectly equal to the transaction of business. Lenoir found her in one of the upper rooms, engaged with one of the maid-servants in unrolling some cloth.

She did not hear him coming in, and he could not help shaking his head as he saw her; a plump, rosy, good-humoured girl of twenty-one, with glossy black hair, and lively black eyes, and a pretty, round, good-tempered face. Oh! if she had but been a boy, he thought, with a deep sigh. Charlotte heard the sigh, and looking up, saw the old man standing in the doorway, with his pen behind his ear, and a woe-begone meaning on his wrinkled face.

"Monsieur Lenoir," she said, knitting her smooth brow into a frown, "do you know that this cloth is moth-eaten?"

Monsieur Lenoir was very sorry to hear it, but begged for five minutes' private conversation with Mademoiselle.

"To be sure," airily replied Charlotte. "Marie, you will fold up that calico, please. I shall be down directly."

Monsieur Lenoir sighed again. His errand was a sad one, but it must be spoken. To his amazement, Charlotte interrupted him at once.

"Thank you," she said, "but please

P 2

tell that Monsieur Roussel that I shall carry on the business myself."

If the pen had not been very firm indeed behind Monsieur Lenoir's ear, it must have dropped at so astounding an announcement. Without seeming to perceive his amazement, as expressed in staring eyes and open mouth, Mademoiselle Morel continued: "Whenever my poor father came to see me, he lamented that I was a girl; so not knowing what might happen, I did my best to qualify myself for business. I learned book-keeping."

" But, Mademoiselle," interrupted Lenoir, " book-keeping is nothing—nothing. You do not know the intricacies of business."

In her turn Mademoiselle Morel interrupted the clerk. She laid her hand upon his arm, and looking in his face, she said, good-humouredly but very firmly :—

" I know good butter, and good flour, and good cloth, and good wares, Monsieur Lenoir, and none but good wares will I keep. My father neither took nor gave credit, I believe. His word also was his bond; he was honourable in his dealings, and prudent in his ventures. What he did, I shall do; and Monsieur Lenoir," she added, feelingly, "no cloth of this texture and this price shall get moth-eaten under my rule. Why," she added, raising her eyebrows, pursing her lips and shaking her young head, "here are several hundred francs lost at the very least."

Monsieur Lenoir stared and was dumb. Remonstrance was useless, and he knew it. Of course this poor, deluded young thing would never get on—never, not even with his assistance—but she had a will of her own, she was of age too, and it was plain that she emerged from her convent with the determination of having her own way henceforward.

Monsieur Lenoir was simply and sadly sceptical, but Verrières was bitterly ironical. It foretold Mademoiselle Morel's downfall, and watched her going down. The process was not a rapid one. Charlotte got on very well. Monsieur Lenoir did the travelling and the going-about, and she stayed at home and minded the business. It was hard for one so young to lead this dull, confined life, and so Charlotte soon found; but pleasure is unknown in Verrières, and she had no choice. Sometimes she wondered if she should go on so till old age, buying and selling, and making money; but she was so far a true daughter of mediæval Verrières, that she never thought of exchanging the dullness of her native place for the gaieties of a large city. Now and then, indeed, she longed for the country, and gardens, and green fields; but she could not have these and attend to business, so she tried to be content with her shop and her store-rooms, and the yard, and the creepers, and to find music in that chink of money which had so long charmed her father's ears. In the meanwhile, Verrières went on wondering how long she would last. At first, Mademoiselle Morel knew nothing of the commotion her unexpected resolve had excited. But by-and-by,

good-natured people, who felt bound to
tell her, let her into the secret. She thus
learned that her downfall, slow, but sure,
was predicted, and that not even in her
own family was a voice raised to prophecy
her success. Louise Roussel, a little
chatterer of some seven years old, whom
Charlotte was very fond of, gave her more
information on that head than she cared
to hear. She came in to her one evening,
flushed and breathless with excitement.

"Oh! cousin," she cried, running up
to Mademoiselle Morel, who was in the
yard watering the creepers, "such news!
My big brother Henri has just arrived."

"Indeed."

"Yes; for a week only, you know.
They all say I am so like him. Am I like
him?" And she raised herself on tiptoe,
and shook her auburn hair, for Charlotte
the better to see the likeness.

Mademoiselle Morel looked down into
the child's bright face.

"Yes, you are like him," she said, ab-
stractedly, and she remained thus, with

the watering-pot in her hand, like one in a dream.

"And they told him about you, you know," pursued Louise; "and papa groaned, and said you would never do. And Uncle Joseph laughed, and said you would never do; and Henri, you know, said, why not? Women do very well in business when they have brains and no heart."

Charlotte was silent; if it were not that she changed colour a little, she looked as if she had not heard the child.

"And Henri is going to Uncle Joseph's, to-night," continued the little thing; "and as he will not be back till Friday, mamma will ask you to come and spend to-morrow's holiday with us. They asked Henri if he would mind seeing you—he said, no; but it would be awkward for a whole day."

Still Charlotte was silent.

"How hot it is under this skylight!" she said at last; "come out with me, Louise." And passing through one of the

outhouses, they came out on the brink of
the river behind it. Charlotte had had a
wooden bench placed there, and of an
evening, when the shop was shut, she
liked to come and sit here and breathe a
little fresh air. It was also a favourite
haunt of Monsieur Lenoir's, who was a
great angler, and who devoted to his
favourite pursuit everything like spare
time. They found him there, standing on
a stone, stiff, straight, and still, like an
old heron watching for his prey. Charlotte sat down on the bench without
speaking to him, and Louise nestled
against her. The evening was very calm
and still. The stream was silvery and
grey; above the willows and aspens on
the opposite bank rose a pale crescent
moon; the lowing of distant cattle came
from remote pastures, and from the neighbouring garden, the gay laughter of the
Roussels. Presently, a boat shot forth,
and turned on the stream. Charlotte saw
that Henri, a strange young man, and
Marie, the elder sister of Louise, were in

it. Marie was laughing very gaily, and half in mirth, half in real fear, she was clinging to her brother.

"Take care," he said gently; "take care." And even as he spoke, he saw Charlotte sitting on the bench, with Louise by her side. He was bare-headed, but he rose and bowed very gravely, then sitting down again he rowed on. The voices lessened, then died away, the boat vanished in a bend of the river, everything was calm and silent, and the stars came out one by one in the deepening blue of the sky, and Charlotte Morel felt very sad and very lonely. But as she rose and went in with Louise, she thought: "I would do it over again."

She took the child to her own house. She found Monsieur Roussel in the garden. He asked her to sit down; and not having any fear of seeing Henri, she complied whilst her uncle resumed his digging.

"And how are you getting on?" he said, after awhile, resting on his spade to address her.

" I am getting on well, uncle, I thank you."

Monsieur Roussel groaned, and shook his head.

" Get married," he said ; " get married, Charlotte."

" I am in no hurry, uncle."

" Well, you did wonderfully well not to take Henri, at least," he said ruefully. " What do you think he came for ?"

Charlotte did not answer.

" Why, to ask me for seven thousand five hundred francs. Neither more nor less. ' What for ?' said I. ' But that he could not tell me,' he replied. Seven thousand five hundred francs !" exclaimed Monsieur Roussel, in pious horror. " That boy will not end well, Charlotte."

Perhaps Charlotte had found to her own cost that one's friends are liberal of such prophecies, for she did not look so horrified as Monsieur Roussel evidently expected.

" You do not mean to say you think that natural ?" he exclaimed, looking injured.

"I think nothing about it, uncle. Where is aunt?"

Madame Roussel now joined them. She, too, was full of the seven thousand five hundred francs.

"You know what Henri came for?" she said, plaintively.

"Yes; uncle has told me. What a fine evening?"

"Will you come and spend to-morrow with us? Henri will not be at home," continued Madame Roussel.

"I am not afraid of Henri," rather proudly replied Charlotte; "but I shall be glad to spend to-morrow with you," she added, with a little sigh, "holidays seem so lonely."

The Verrières fashion of spending holiday is a dull one.

A good dinner, a walk in the garden, and a round game of cards in the evening, was all the entertainment that Madame Roussel thought needful for her family. A thunderstorm interfered with one part of the programme: the garden was inaccessible. The dinner and the round game remained. Very long and wearisome seemed the dinner to Charlotte, who did not care for good cheer; and the evening was not much better. She soon lost all her counters, and was henceforth out of the game. Whilst the others played on, she leaned back in her chair, listening to the wind, which was rising, and to the rain that now beat wildly against the window-panes. Monsieur Roussel was peering at the cards through his gold spectacles; Marie showed her hand to her mother, who nodded and smiled; and little Louise, leaning her head heavily against Charlotte, was falling asleep. Mademoiselle Morel looked at them a little wistfully. There is pleasure and also pain in beholding a family circle when we are ourselves alone.

"If they had not asked me to join them," thought Charlotte, "I must have sat alone in my room this evening; and, because they asked me, he left the house —just as he left Verrières on my account four years ago. They do not seem to miss him much; and yet they surely care more about him than they care about me?"

A violent knocking at the front door roused her from her reverie. She looked up, with a start, and found the notary, his wife, and daughter exchanging alarmed glances.

"Why, what can have happened?" began Monsieur Roussel. "Surely—"

Here the knocking was repeated more violently than before, and this time the shuffling step of the servant, coming from the back of the house, said that she was hastening to give the impatient visitor admittance. They heard the front door opening, and some one rushed in; then the door of the room in which they were sitting burst open, and Monsieur Joseph Roussel broke in upon them, with wild looks, wet garments, and a dripping umbrella.

"My money!" he gasped. "My money!" he shouted, recovering breath, and striking the floor with his umbrella. "Where is my money?"

They looked at him aghast. Monsieur Roussel remained with the uplifted card he was going to play in his hand, and stared at his brother with open mouth and eyes.

"I tell you I want my money," doggedly resumed Joseph. "I want my seven thousand five hundred francs."

"Seven thousand five hundred francs!" repeated the notary, turning livid, and a dreadful light seeming to break upon him as he heard the amount of the sum.

"Yes, seven thousand five hundred francs," sternly said Henri's uncle and godfather—"seven thousand five hundred francs, which were taken out of my desk this afternoon when Henri was in the house—do you hear?" and he rolled his eyes about and winked at them all with terrible significance.

Monsieur Roussel tried to speak, but words would not come to him. He sank forward on the table, and with his head lying there, uttered a deep, heart-broken groan. Madame Roussel raised her hands to heaven, and uttered a despairing cry.

" We are ruined—ruined, disgraced, outdone !" she said, wildly; and falling back into her chair, she went into hysterics; upon which Marie began sobbing violently, and little Louise, who had been staring round her in dismay, uttered a succession of piercing shrieks. Charlotte alone preserving some presence of mind, ran to her aunt's assistance, and endeavoured to calm her. Joseph Roussel looked around him in grim and gloomy triumph, winking rapidly.

" Spare the rod and spoil the child," he said; " I knew how it would be—I always said so."

" For heaven's sake, have mercy on us !" cried Monsieur Roussel, looking up, wildly. " Perhaps—perhaps Henri did not do it."

" Then who did ?" angrily retorted his brother. " Do you want to cheat me out of my money, eh? You told me yourself he came to borrow seven thousand five hundred francs—did you not? Well, I tell you that I left Henri alone in the room with my desk, and when I came back at the end of a quarter of an hour, Henri had vanished, the key, which I had forgotten on the table, was in the desk, and seven thousand five hundred francs in notes were gone. But if you think that I am going to bear with that loss just because Henri is my nephew and godson, you are very much mistaken, all of you," added Monsieur Joseph Roussel, glaring at the dismayed family, and striking the floor again with his umbrella.

" Henri shall return that money : he only meant to borrow it, of course," agitatedly said the notary. " But he shall return it, Joseph."

" And do you suppose I am going to wait till he returns my money ?" exclaimed Joseph Roussel, looking indignant and amazed at the suggestion. " What brought me here, pray ?"

" And how do I know that my son took your money ?" asked Monsieur Roussel, with a feeble effort at scepticism.

"Did I not tell you so?" cried his brother, enraged.

"Well, but did you see him doing it?" desperately asked Monsieur Roussel— "did you see him?"

Joseph Roussel stared till his eyes seemed ready to start out of their sockets.

"See him!" he at length gasped forth— "see him open my desk, and take out my hard-earned money, seven thousand five hundred francs!—you ask me if I saw him doing that? No, sir," he indignantly exclaimed, answering his own question, "I did not see him, because he took care not to do it till my back was turned. But I can tell you what—Jean, my servant, heard and saw. He saw your son Henri at the post-offiee, handing over to the post-mistress a letter with five blue seals— five blue seals—and declaring it to be worth seven thousand five hundred francs! What do you think of that?"

The notary groaned. "For heaven's sake have mercy on me!" he said, piteously.

"I want my money, sir; my money!"

" You shall have it, though it will half ruin me," distractedly said Monsieur Roussel; " but keep it quiet—oh, keep it quiet !"

" And what did I come here for but to keep it quiet ?" screamed Joseph, at the pitch of his voice; " what did I come here for ?"

" It will ruin me," said Henri's father, despairingly ; " it will ruin me !"

On hearing this, Madame Roussel burst into tears, and with many piteous sobs she asked why her children were to be plundered ·for Henri's misdeeds. Her husband heard her with a dull, vacant stare of misery. There is a tragic hour in most lives, however tame and common-place may seem their current, and that tragic hour had come to him. Grief and despair gave a terrible meaning to his little peevish face, and Charlotte's heart sank within her as she heard him mutter in a low, dull voice, " I will not be disgraced. On the day when this is known in Ver-rières, I shall just go down the garden, and make a hole in the water : I will not be disgraced."

Even as he uttered the words, the door opened and Henri, who had come back in his boat and walked up the garden, entered the room.

" Cards," he said, carelessly, " cards— who wins ?"

No one answered. He gave a sharp look round the room, and at once his careless look vanished. But he did not speak. He stood without uttering one word, evidently waiting. His father rose.

" Henri," he said, sternly, "you sent off seven thousand five hundred francs to Paris to-day."

Henri looked thunderstruck.

" I did," he replied, at length.

" To whom ?"

" I cannot tell."

" From whom did you get that money ?"

" I cannot tell."

The young man spoke very sullenly, and looked black as night at that cross-examination.

" You must get that money back," said his father, trying to speak composedly, though he was deadly pale : " for your uncle," he added, pointing to the dark part of the room where Joseph Roussel stood leaning on his umbrella, " your uncle had his desk opened to-day, and seven thousand five hundred francs taken from it."

Henri gave a sudden start, and turned dreadfully pale.

" You did not think I should miss it so soon, did you ?" asked his Uncle Joseph, nodding grimly at him ; " but you had scarcely turned your back on the house when I wanted some money, and found out that my seven thousand five hundred francs were gone. Thank your stars that I am your godfather as well as your uncle," he added, in a menacing voice. " Thank your stars, I say !"

Henri sank on a chair, and thence looked at him, then from him to his father. At first it seemed as if his words would not pass his white lips. When he spoke

at length, it was to address the notary
and say :

" Father, what do you say to this ?"

Monsieur Roussel raised his trembling
hand towards him.

" God forgive you, Henri," he said, in
a broken voice.

Henri leaped up from the chair on
which he was sitting ; his blue eyes flashed
like fire, his pale face grew still paler with
wrath, as iron is at its hottest when it is
whitest, and in a voice of thunder he
cried :

" Father ! father ! what do you mean ?"

" Do !—threaten your father after dis-
honouring him," cried Madame Roussel,
starting up in mingled fear and hate.

Henri gave his step-mother a look of indignation and scorn ; but before he could
open his lips to reply, Charlotte went up
to the notary, and laying her hand on his
arm, she said in a low, indignant voice,
whilst her other outstretched hand pointed
to Henri Roussel, " Uncle, uncle, do you
not see that your son is innocent ?"

" Innocent !" gasped the notary, staring round the room, " how so ?"

" How so ! look at him and see it.
Henri Roussel is innocent—I tell you he
is innocent," she added, her eyes flashing
with generous indignation, " and that you
ought all to die with shame at having
doubted him."

" Yes, I am innocent," sternly said the
young man ; " and, what is more, I can
prove it. That money which uncle so
kindly accuses me of having taken from
his desk, I already had when I saw him.
I borrowed it on my vineyard above Verrières. Ask Farmer Grangé, and see if
he will deny it."

" Then who took my money ?" cried
Monsieur Joseph Roussel, looking very
wild.

" That is your business, not mine,"
bitterly replied the young man; then
looking round him he added : " I have
learned this evening what trust in my
honour I may expect in this house. Let
none of you wonder that I shall hence-

forth make my home among strangers. I leave Verrières this very night—now, this moment, and it will be strange indeed if I ever set foot in it again."

He looked round the room once more ; then going straight up to the spot where Charlotte stood alone :

" God bless you !" he said, with much emotion, " God bless you !"

She did not answer. She stood there before him, passive, and like one in a dream. He said no more, but turned away, and was gone. As the door closed upon him, as they heard his step rapidly going up the staircase, the notary, re-covering from his amazement, turned angrily on his brother :

" How dare you come with your cock-and-bull stories to me ?" he cried, with fury. " How dare you accuse my son of robbery ?"

Monsieur Joseph Roussel slapped his forehead. Then a sudden light seemed to break upon him.

" I know who did it," he cried ; " I

know!" And he rushed out of the house like one distracted.

The notary threw himself down on a chair, and addressing his wife, said, very ruefully:

"Louise, you should have told me not to believe it—you should have told me."

Madame Roussel raised her pocket-handkerchief to her eyes, and speaking from behind it, said, in a melancholy voice:

"It all falls upon me because I am not his mother."

Charlotte signed to Marie to follow her out of the room. When they both stood outside the door, she whispered:

"Go and beg of your brother not to leave the house to-night."

"I dare not," replied Marie, whose eyes were red with weeping; "Henri never minds me."

"Try, Marie—try," urged Charlotte.

The girl went reluctantly, and very anxiously Charlotte waited for her at the foot of the staircase. Marie soon came down again; Henri's door was locked, and he had refused to admit her. Madame Roussel, who now joined them, heard this, and looked piteously at her niece.

" Do try, Charlotte," she said, " do try."

" I !" said Charlotte, with a start.

" Yes, do. My poor husband is broken-hearted, but will not say a word to keep him, and Henri would not mind me ; but he will at least hear you. If he would only stay to-night ! Do try, Charlotte ! You can go and sit upstairs, and speak to him when he is coming down."

She put a light in her niece's hand, and Charlotte took it like one in a dream. She went up to the room on the first floor, and sat down leaving the door open. Everything looked very gaunt and dreary in the pale light of the wax candle, burning quietly on the table. The tall, ledger-like books, the dull iron safe, the stiff, black chairs, were very grim and forbidding of aspect ; but Charlotte, if she saw, did not heed them. She was listening to sounds in the room above, sounds of hurried footsteps and moving furniture, which ended at length in the unlocking of a door and a step coming down the staircase. Without leaving her chair, or even looking round, Charlotte said, in a low voice :

" Henri !"

She spoke so low that he might not have heard her ; but he did. He came in at once. He threw the carpet-bag he was carrying on the floor ; he drew a chair near hers, and sitting down upon it, he took the hand that hung loosely in the folds of her black dress, and he raised it to his lips.

" God bless you for your faith in me !" he said, in a low voice; " I shall never forget it—never."

" I trust you are not going," she said, without looking round at him. " Your father, your mother, are deeply grieved."

" Do not believe it," he interrupted, bitterly ; " they never loved me, or they could not have thought me guilty so readily. What have I ever done to deserve such an insult as this ?"

" Ah ! nothing—nothing indeed," Char-

lotte could not help saying; "but they repent it: forgive them."

"Willingly; but I will not live with
them.   This evening has burned itself into
my very soul. It has shown me two things
it is not in my power to forget—their
doubt, and your faith in my honour.   He
rose as he said this.

"Pray, do stay," she urged.

"Stay! What for?" he asked moodily.
"They will suspect me next for that money; they will want to know what I am
doing with it and if I do not tell—and I
will not tell them—they will shake their
heads, and say, 'Henri is going to ruin.
We always said so.'"

Charlotte was silent.

"But you must think no harm of me
for that," he resumed, eagerly; "that
money is to save a friend from disgrace. I
run no risk; I have security to double the
amount I lend; but to have it known that
he borrows would ruin him, and ruin him
so thoroughly that I should not have told
you so much, only I could not bear you

to think, as they will be sure to say, that I am a spendthrift and a profligate."

" Pray, do stay," she said, again.

" I cannot. You have been very good to me this evening—better than I deserve; but I cannot stay."

" Why so ?"

" Do not ask me." His voice shook as he uttered the words.

For the first time Charlotte turned her face towards him. Their looks met : their eyes were very dim with tears; yet each read the same story in the other's gaze. In a moment the tale was told, understood, and firmly believed in for ever.

" Then you like me—you do like me !" cried Henri, amazed and delighted.

" A little, but very little," she replied, smiling demurely; " for, if you go, how can I like you ?"

" Ah, how can I go now !" he exclaimed, overjoyed.

All the wisdom of Verrières went distracted on the day when Charlotte and Henri's banns were published. A nice mess of poor Monsieur Morel's money those two would make, and a nice life they would lead. It is mortifying to record it, but the wisdom of Verrières was again all wrong. The business flourished in the hands of the young pair, and Charlotte's faith in him was the spell which bound the dragon of Henri's temper for ever. Never once—and three years have passed since their wedding-day—did that fierce dragon waken when she was concerned, though truth compels us to say that Henri's uncle and godfather once or twice found how that same dragon was not always sleeping.

The unfortunate gentleman's seven thousand five hundred francs were never recovered, and the mystery of their disappearance promises to become one of the legends of Verrières.

Mimi's Sin.

N old French Countess, who had
bright eyes and a lively tongue,
once said to me: " I never read
stories of any kind. I never
read any since I was a child, when I read
the fairy tales, of course. I maintain
that they are or ought to be sufficient to
the wants of a novel-reading generation;
for, you see, fairy tales are simply delicious. They are like life, in so far as
they deal with men and women; but oh!
how unlike it in the ultimate fate of heroes
and heroines, in retribution and justice.

Here are no oppressed innocents sinking under the weight of their troubles, no triumphant avengers waiting for punishment in the next world. We can take up a fairy tale in most delightful security concerning its ending, and perhaps its great attraction is that it never deceives or disappoints us."

"Oh! but remember Blue Beard; remember——"

"Exceptions," she interrupted; "the genuine fairy tale is never tragic, never gloomy. It is full of romance, full of poetry, and, of course, full of love."

"Unreal——" I began, but was again interrupted.

"Unreal?" almost screamed the Countess, quite forgetting that she had just been pleading for the unreality of fairy tales as their great attraction. "Why, there is nothing more real in life than these old stories. I meet the mat every corner. 'There you are,' I say to them; 'I know you. There you are, old friends.'"

But when I asked the Countess to prove

the truth of this bold assertion, she remained mute. She turned up her eyes, tapped her foot, reckoned on her fingers, and at length so far confessed herself conquered that she acknowledged not remembering any particular fairy tale in real life just then, for you see there was ever some unfortunate hitch. Either the heroine was plain, or the evil fairy, who is always so signally conquered, proved too strong, or the prince was faithless, or, in short, one or the other of the essentials which go to make up a real fairy tale was wanting.

"It is all our unbelief," impatiently said the Countess; "if we only had the childish faith, fairy tales would grow around us like mushrooms. Taking it for granted that you will give me unlimited credence, I will tell you a real story, which is as good as a fairy tale in some things, though it belongs to no established type:

"When I was in Normandy ten years ago, I had to call on Madame de Grandsire, a widowed lady with five children, heavy debts, and very little money. I set forth on a grey afternoon in October, with tempestuous clouds drifting in the sky. The sea, dark and livid, spread far away to my left; to the right the Château of Grandsire rose above yellow autumn woods, a grey old mansion, flanked with four turrets quietly going to ruin beneath a cloak of green ivy, and the nearer the carriage drew to it the more dilapidated the old place looked. You see, the Grandsires had been very brilliant and very gay under the ancient régime. They had gambled, they had given delicious little suppers, they had flirted with philosophy, and vied with court favourites. To crown all, they had emigrated, and been guillotined, and had forgotten to worship the rising sun of imperial greatness; so when they came back to the old country, they found that they had lost some of the best feathers in their wing—feathers which now nodded in plebeian caps over plebeian brows, and which the old Grandsire eagle must never again call his own.

" No wonder that the château was going to ruins; no wonder that the garden was wild and uncared for; no wonder that the old servant who showed me up a gaunt oaken staircase wore so shabby a livery. Least wonder of all was it that the salon into which I was ushered was so vast, so cold and bare. I had just time to see the dreary range of windows with a dismal prospect of the yellow woods—just time to note the scanty furniture of faded crimson velvet, and to catch a glimpse of Madame de Grandsire and her children seated at the farthest end of the room, when, even before the old man-servant could utter my name, the lady of the house exclaimed, breathlessly : ' Shut the door !'

" I looked up for the bird or cat or dog whose escape was apprehended; but though I was conscious that something had rushed past me, and was now darting down the staircase, I saw nothing, and did not know what sort of a creature it was.

" ' She is gone,' resignedly said Madame de Grandsire. 'I beg your pardon, my

R 2

dear Countess, but a saint would lose patience with Mimi. I can only keep her in by dressing her in boy's clothes, and I cannot always do that—can I ?'

" I thought at first the offender was one of Madame de Grandsire's three daughters ; but no : there they were, models of youthful propriety, each sitting primly on her chair, each looking virtuously indignant at Mimi's sin. This Mimi was a little penniless orphan, whom the late Monsieur de Grandsire, on a plea that she was distantly related to him, had brought home from a remote province. ' As if we wanted a sixth child !' plaintively exclaimed Madame de Grandsire, who, as I soon found, was always deploring her poverty.

" Réné, her eldest son, was standing in one of the deep windows. He was a tall, grave lad of seventeen, dark, and very handsome, but with a premature look of care on his face. On hearing his mother's speech, he turned slowly from the autumn prospect at which he had been gazing, and, colouring deeply as he spoke, he said in a low, displeased voice :

" ' Are we so poor that we cannot afford to keep the child ?'

" ' Indeed we are,' tartly replied Madame de Grandsire. ' Debts, a château, five children to rear, dress, and educate, and no money.'

" Réné's dark eye flashed, his lips quivered; and, unable to bear exposure of the Grandsire poverty, he left the room.

" ' Réné is fond of Mimi ?' I said.

" ' He detests her," replied Madame de Grandsire. ' No one can like so perverse a child.'

" ' Oh, no one !' echoed Mesdemoiselles de Grandsire, looking very demure.

" ' It is pride,' resumed their mother. ' Réné would starve rather than one of the Grandsire blood and name should want. He is the proudest boy.'

" I liked that pride, but I wished it had been tempered with a ray of love for poor little Mimi. This, however, was impossible, according to Madame de Grandsire. A wilder little creature, one less amenable to love and law, than Mimi had never existed.

" 'You remember the sea-bath ?' she added, turning to her eldest daughter, who raised her eyes and shook her head: 'whilst my children bathed decorously, Mimi acted like a young barbarian, swimming like a fish and screaming like a seabird. I do believe she would have been drowned but for Réné. Two days after this she was missing. She did not appear at luncheon ; she did not come in to dinner ; and where do you suppose that Réné found her ? Fast asleep in a tree. The creature must have been a bird before she was born a human child, and so she has kept the tendency to perch. I locked her up in the dining-room yesterday for misbehaviour, and when I sent Réné for her he found her sitting on the marble mantelpiece ! My only remedy is to dress her in André's clothes, but that makes her frantic with shame, and Réné will not have it.'

" Violent screams from the garden broke on Madame de Grandsire's lamentations. We all rushed to the windows, and saw Réné, like a young Romulus, bearing

away a childish Sabine with golden hair,
and whose hands and feet were very busy
with his person, till they both vanished in
the house.

"' I dare say she was in the river, and
that he took her out,' said Madame de
Grandsire. 'She scratches, kicks, and
bites him; she pulls his hair, she tears
his clothes, and he endures it all; it is his
pride.'

"I condoled with Madame de Grandsire; but in my heart I sypathized with
that little wicked Mimi. I liked her
superfluous vitality, just as I liked that
young Réné's pride; just, too, as I dis-
liked the decorum of his three prim sisters,
and cared nothing about the dull insignifi-
cance of the younger boy André, whose
garments sinning Mimi wore every now
and then. She must have been a naughty
child, indeed, for she was always out of
the way—on the wing, if I may so speak
—when I called on Madame de Grandsire,
and as I soon left Normandy, and did not
return for some years, Mimi was in her
teens when I saw her first.

She was standing on the perron of the
old château—alas! it looked more dilapidated than ever—with the warm sunshine
pouring full on her young face and bare
head; and though Mimi wore the simplest
of black dresses, and the plainest of white
collars, she looked the prettiest creature
I had ever seen. She was about seventeen then, a slight, young thing, with a
sweet wayward face, dark eyes, soft and
bright, and hair which rippled like gold
in the light of the setting sun. Seeing her
so pretty, and, as it seemed to me, so
winning, I at once wove a little romance,
in which this fascinating Mimi was Juliet
to Réné's Romeo; but Madame de Grandsire's first words dispelled the illusion.
Mimi glided up the oaken staircase like a
bright sunbeam, showed me into the
dreary, faded salon, then vanished. My
friend, after the usual polite inquiries, at
once began to complain. The debts had
been paid; but at what cost, at what
sacrifice! Her daughters were unmarried,
and Mimi was worse than ever. She did

not perch in trees now, but she spent her life in mischief. The jarring between her and Réné was incessant. She could get on with Mimi, and so could her daughters —André had long been dead; but between Mimi and Réné it was war from morning till night—on Mimi's side, of course, for nothing could exceed Réné's dignified courtesy spite all Mimi's irritating ways. Mademoiselle Jerôme wondered at his goodness. To this lady Réné, it seemed, was engaged. Mademoiselle Jerôme, as I further learned, was a plebeian heiress of twenty-two, much admired for her bright eyes and her 500,000 francs. Réné and she had exchanged their hearts at a ball, and they were to be married next month, and this marriage was to be the making of the family. Réné was an excellent farmer, but he had little land, and no capital. His wife's money would work wonders. It would rebuild the château, refurnish the salon, improve the land, and be trebled in no time. Besides, Mademoiselle Jerôme had an uncle who was deep in all sorts of lucrative undertakings, and who was to make them all rich by some magical process or other. No wonder that so potent a lady's comments on Mimi's behaviour should be recorded! Poor naughty little Mimi! what was to become of her, if, when they all lived together in the château, the rich bride took a dislike to her? I could hear her trilling away in the garden below, and her voice was so sweet that I could not think there was much harm in her; but I stayed to dinner, and Mimi's behaviour, I am sorry to say, quite bore out the truth of Madame de Grandsire's statement, viz., that Mimi had left off perching in trees, and other indecorous pastimes, for indoor mischief of a much more dangerous nature. When I saw her sitting by Réné's side, and looked at these two so unlike and yet so handsome, I could not help regretting my day-dream; but when I heard Mimi—her real name was Amélie—so sly, so wicked, so demure, probing Réné to the quick, never sparing him a thrust or a sting; and when I saw the flash of his dark eye or the ill-repressed working of his lip, whilst he bore it all in dignified silence, never relaxing one moment from his grave courtesy towards the silly girl, who owed the very clothes she wore to his generosity, I felt that my day-dream was best left in abeyance.

"What I saw then, I saw every time these two were together in my presence. With the three prim daughters of the house, Mimi got on so far that she did not meddle with them; and if I might form any opinion from their lofty looks, they were wholly unconscious that such a person as Mimi existed; to their mother she was respectful; to Réné alone her behaviour was intolerable. Now and then he lost patience, and gave her a sharp rebuff, but, as a rule, he endured her naughtiness with an outward forbearance, which probably concealed much inward wrath. How Mimi fared with Mademoiselle Jerôme, or rather, I should say, how that lady fared at her hands, I should

much have liked to see, but, to my great
regret, I never had the opportunity.

" I led a lonely life just then, with some
cares and troubles to keep me company.
I used to sit and brood over these of an
evening, after the fashion of women, and
I was rather apt to look at the logs blazing
on the hearth—autumn had set in early—
and to listen to the low moaning of the
wind, and make myself miserable. I was
thus engaged one evening, when I received a hurried note from Madame de
Grandsire, entreating me to come to her
immediately. What could have happened?
I wondered all the way, for I went at
once, and I was wondering still when I
walked up the oaken staircase and entered
the dreary old salon. It was almost dark;
a lonely wax-light in a tall silver candlestick, and a low fire dying away on the
broad hearth, were not calculated to dispel
the gloom of that ghostly apartment. I
thought it was vacant, but as I drew near
the fireplace I became aware of Mimi's
presence. She sat, as I had often seen

her sitting, on a low hassock. Her hands
were clasped around her knees, her dark
eyes were bent on the fire, and its ruddy
light played brightly in the waves of her
golden hair and on her fair young face, so
sweet though so wayward. She never
moved or looked round on hearing me.

" ' Good evening,' said I.

" ' Good evening,' she answered, shortly.

" ' How is Madame de Grandsire ?' I
asked, not disheartened.

" ' All wrong, and so is Réné, and so am
I ; we are all wrong !' and Mimi uttered
the dearest little groan, and there were
tears in her dark eyes as she spoke.

" Before I could question further, the
door of the salon opened, and Madame de
Grandsire and her three daughters entered
the room, with the longest of long faces
and the most woebegone of looks. At
once Madame de Grandsire told me
what had happened. Mademoiselle
Jerôme had broken her engagement with
Réné, returned his letters, asked for her
portrait, and refused to see him. ' In

short,' exclaimed Madame de Grandsire, bursting into tears, 'Réné is broken-hearted, and we are ruined for ever!'

" The red eyes and red noses of Réné's three sisters showed in what light they considered this calamity, and a little snivelling sound from Mimi's hassock betrayed her sympathy in the universal grief. I was very sorry, and I was much perplexed. My first words were to ask what reason Mademoiselle Jerôme assigned for such conduct.

" 'None,' plaintively replied Madame de Grandsire, and her daughters echoed 'None,' and added, 'If we only knew why.' I have a great horror of meddling in affairs of that kind, yet I was going to volunteer my services, when Réné's entrance checked the words on my lips. I suppose the young fellow was much smitten: he certainly looked very much cut up. He gave us all a quick glance, guessed what we had been talking about, and said, in a vexed tone: 'My dear mother, why trouble the Countess with that matter? It must be borne.'

" 'My dear Réné,' I answered, my generous wish to assist him getting strengthened as I saw the grief of the family, and felt what a blow this was to them all, 'let me do something. Let me at least try to learn Mademoiselle Jerôme's reason; perhaps it is one which you can remove with a word.'

" Réné looked irresolute; he took several turns up and down the long room; pride and love were struggling in his heart; but when he paused before me, with his pale face rather flushed, and his haughty glance downcast, I knew that love had prevailed. He was going to speak, when a loud sob from Mimi's hassock startled us all.

" 'Oh, I am so—so very sorry!' she moaned. 'It—it was I who did it all!'

" I looked at Réné; he seemed petrified.

" 'You?' he said at length, casting a searching look down upon her. 'You? —and, pray, how so?'

" But Mimi was weeping piteously, and could not speak at once. At length it came out, with many sobs:

"'I told Mademoseille Jerôme, that—that you said—there—there never was a more beautiful creature than—than Madame David.'

"There surely never was a more perverse little creature than this. Every one knew that Madame David, the beautiful young widow, was Mary Stuart to Mademoiselle Jerôme's Elizabeth. Every one knew that to praise Madame David to Mademoiselle Jerôme was to forfeit favour for ever with that lady, and, of course, Réné had never meant his words to be repeated. He turned on Mimi with flashing eyes and quivering lips.

"'Why did you say this?' he asked, vehemently.

"Falsehood was not Mimi's sin. Her reply was deplorably candid.

"'Because I knew it would worry you. But, oh!' she plaintively added, 'I did not think it would make you lose the five hundred thousand francs.'

"The loss of Mademoiselle Jerôme's heart Mimi, it was plain, thought very little of. Réné gave her an indignant look; I believe he was too angry to speak; but Madame de Grandsire's wrath laboured under no such impediment. She was a weak woman, and the weak under great provocation become violent. She now forgot her good breeding completely.

" ' You little serpent!' she cried, starting up in burning anger; 'were you received and sheltered in this house to become our ruin ?'

" On hearing the maternal signal, the three Mesdemoiselles de Grandsire joined in full cry: ' Ingrate !' ' Wretch !' ' Little monster !' burst from their lips.

" Never before had Mimi received such treatment. She had been scolded as a child, reprimanded as a girl, and never loved, but she had not been told she ate the bread of charity—she had not been insulted and humiliated. She became pale as death when this fierce storm broke over her, and turning her frightened look around, saw but one with whom she could take refuge, the very one whom she had most deeply offended.

"'Oh, Réné!' she cried, cowering by his side, and looking piteously in his face; 'you know I did not mean to ruin you, you know I did not.'

"Réné, recovering from the astonishment into which so unexpected an outburst had thrown him, gently laid his hand on Mimi's shoulder, and, looking at his mother, said very gravely:

"'My dear mother, allow me to remind you that Mademoiselle Amélie de Grandsire's position requires, nay, exacts, the strictest courtesy at our hands. She has sinned very deeply, but more through heedlessness than through malice.'

"'Oh, pray do not call me Mademoiselle Amélie de Grandsire!' entreated Mimi.

"But Réné resumed, with cutting politeness: 'I am sure Mademoiselle Amélie de Grandsire will never act so again.'

"'Oh, Réné! do not be so angry,' said Mimi.

"But, with the same killing courtesy,

Réné declared he was not angry; and having thus crushed Mimi much more effectually than either his sisters or his mother, he let her go back weeping to her place, and resumed his.

" I tried to mend matters by offering to see Mademoiselle Jerôme, but Réné would not hear of it. He had said that Madame David was the most beautiful creature he had ever seen, and if he had thus displeased Mademoiselle Jerôme, he was quite willing to abide by the consequences of his words. His tone was so peremptory, that I felt silenced. My presence, after what had passed, was useless and awkward. I rose to go. Réné showed me downstairs himself.

" As we reached the door, we heard something rustling down the staircase. We both looked round, and, by the faint light of the lamp, we saw Mimi—Mimi, pale, and in tears. She went up to Réné and clung to him.

" ' Do not call me Mademoiselle Amélie

s 2

de Grandsire !' she entreated. ' I cannot bear it.'

" ' I shall certainly never call you anything else,' he very coldly answered.

" ' You will not call me Mimi?' she said, impetuously.

" ' Never !' he replied, inexorably.

" ' Then I shall never enter this house again,' cried Mimi; and before we were aware of her intention, she had darted through the open door into the dark, wet night—it was raining hard without.

" ' Excuse me,' hurriedly said Réné, ' she will get her death of cold if I do not catch her.' And he, too, was gone.

" Mimi was light as a bird, and I suppose she was already very far, for Réné's hasty steps sounded fainter and fainter, then ceased to be heard, and still he did not return. The rain was over, the moon struggled in the cloudy sky, and shone dimly over the wet garden. The carriage was waiting for me, but I could not bear to go; nay, in my anxiety to know the end, I went down the steps, and walked

a little way along the gravelled path. A
sound of voices soon reached my ear. I
stood still, and, in the quiet night, I heard
Mimi saying vehemently : 'I can bear
anything from them, but from you, Réné,
nothing—nothing.'

" 'Hush !' gently replied Réné's deeper
tones. 'You know very well I always do
end by forgiving you—whatever you do.'

" 'Oh! but you looked so pale and
angry,' ejaculated Mimi.

" 'And you, like a naughty bird, must
needs want to fly away from your cage.
Your hair is all wet.'

" 'I shall never do it again,' penitently
said Mimi. 'Oh, Réné, how good—how
very good you have always been to me !'

" And Mimi began to cry with gratitude
and remorse, I suppose. I suppose, too,
that Réné did his best to comfort her, but
I did not wait to learn the result of his
efforts. You see they were young, and
could afford to cool their quick, warm
blood in the damp night air, but I was
getting chill, and laboured under no such

necessity. Indeed, a severe attack of rheumatism, which kept me a prisoner for several weeks, was the consequence of Mimi's escapade that night, or, perhaps I should rather say, of my own curiosity.

"When at length I got well again, and drove off one evening to dine with my friends, Mimi was the first person I saw. We met on the staircase, and I was struck at once with her altered looks. I thought some new calamity had happened. Oh no! dolefully replied Mimi, but Mademoiselle Jerôme had married the Count d'Epinay that morning. This accounted sufficiently for Madame de Grandsire's despondency at dinner, and the gloomy faces of her three daughters. The meal was a dull one. Mimi looked oppressed with grief, and Réné alone maintained the usual dignified gravity of his demeanour. Mimi was the first to leave the table; the poor child could scarcely keep in her tears. Madame de Grandsire, who felt unwell, retired to her room, and I followed her, to administer such consolation as suited the occasion. At length I left her, and went down.

" Mesdemoiselles de Grandsire were probably mourning together over the ruins of their hopes, for I did not find them in the salon. The solitary wax-light was burning faintly in the tall silver candlestick on the table; and far away the low wood fire shed its ruddy glow upon the hearth. In its light I saw them both sitting there—Mimi and Réné, one on her low hassock, the other on one of the carved oak chairs, side by side, and hand in hand. I saw and heard them, but I don't think they either saw or heard me.

" ' You are sure you have forgiven me ?' Mimi was saying, and I fancied that penitent tears were sparkling in the dark eyes raised towards his bending face.

" ' Quite sure,' he replied, in his grave, kind way.

" ' And that you will never remember it against me ?'

" ' Never !' said Réné. He seemed to

hesitate; then suddenly stooping, he laid his lips gently, but very tenderly, it seemed to me, on Mimi's golden hair.

" Mimi took this strictly as a forgiving, reconciliating kiss, for when I came forward she said, eagerly :

" ' Oh ! Comtesse, you do not know how good Réné is to me.'

" I replied rather drily, that Réné was very kind, and that I knew it. And Réné coloured, and bit his lip, and gave me a doubtful look. He need not have feared me. I could not be very angry with him, poor young fellow. I am sure he meant to be very wise, but Fate was too much for him. He could have resisted Mimi, charming and naughty though she was, if the unkindness of his mother and sisters had not thrown her upon him. If he was not gentle and tender to her, how would she fare ? if he did not love her a little, who would ? I saw a good deal of the family about this time, and I wondered at their folly and their blindness. By always attacking Mimi, they compelled Réné to defend her; by bringing up all her faults, they made him feel and see that Mimi was young, pretty, and, spite her waywardness —now much subdued--amiable and loving. But though he was very kind, kinder than was wise for either, he was not always with his young relation. Réné had a good deal to do and see to, and whilst he was away the war against Mimi went on, rather cruelly at times. She bore it bravely; she never complained to Réné; but she got so pale and thin, that I at length asked her to come and spend some time with me, by way of change. She accepted eagerly, and within a few days Mimi had got back her rosy cheeks and her bright eyes.

" Réné came to see us daily. Mimi's face grew radiant whenever he entered the room; but though Réné had not the fortitude to deny himself these visits, they did not make him happy. Mimi had no wishes and no hopes; but Réné, who knew what ailed him, found it hard, I dare say, to curb his. The sad way in which he looked at this young girl, when she was not observing him, went to my very heart. "Oh! to be a good fairy, I thought, and to bless these two!

"Matters had been going on so for some time, when Réné came in one evening wet and tired. He looked very blank on finding me alone. Mimi was confined to her room with a bad cold, and I told him so at once. Réné became uneasy. Was I sure it was only a cold? Quite sure, I replied; then I suddenly added:

"'Réné, you are in love with Mimi.'

"The colour deepened in Réné's dark cheek, but he was too proud and too loyal to deny.

"'Yes,' he said, a little desperately, 'I am; but what about it? I shall never marry her.'

"'Would she not have you, Réné?'

"'I shall never ask her,' he answered gloomily.

"'Why not?'

"'How can I?' he exclaimed, impatiently. 'I am poor, and she is penniless. My mother and my three sisters, poor

things, will never forgive her Mademoiselle Jerôme's five hundred thousand
francs, and I cannot leave them for her.
Suppose I take my share, and bid them
take theirs, I thereby condemn them to
penury, to ruin perhaps, for what do they
know about farming? and I cannot keep
a wife and a family on what is left to me.
Oh! if I were not tied to the Grandsire
property by honour and duty!' exclaimed
the poor young man, starting up and
walking up and down the room in a fever;
'if I could only earn money in some way
or other, and marry my little Mimi some
day! But I cannot—I cannot.'

"I confess I thought so too. I confess
that I saw no issue to Réné's troubles. I
could not advise him to marry Mimi,
and condemn himself to poverty and domestic discord. I could only advise him
to try and forget her. But Réné shook
his head as he sat down once more. Forget Mimi! no, he could not do that.

"'It was her being so naughty did it
all,' he said, with a heavy sigh. 'She

was so sorry, and my sisters, poor things, were so unkind. I had to take her part and defend her. I pitied her from my heart, and pity turned into love before I knew how or why; and now I cannot conquer it. I think of Mimi morning, noon, and night. I think of her as she is; so pretty, so poor, so charming, spite all her faults. How can I forget her, when the only happiness she can hope for in this world must all come to her through me? I am father and brother to her, as you know. She is what the world would call a burden upon me; no man will ever come to woo and take her away. Who has seen, who knows, and who, alas! would have her? I am her first, and I shall be Mimi's last lover; and yet I must never say to her " Mimi, I love you very dearly." I must not even try to make her fond of me, though I cannot help seeing that it would be very easy to do so. When my mother and my sisters have got reconciled to this last matter, she must come back to us and to the old life. And I must go on loving her and not telling it; till, may be some day when I am a grey old bachelor, and she is a little old maid, I shall say to her, " Mimi, you never knew it—but I loved you all these years." '

" Réné said all this very ruefully, bending forward with his feet on the fender and his eyes on the fire. This silent celibacy was not a cheerful prospect for a man of twenty-five. I thought he would find it hard, and I said so. Yes, it was hard, he confessed it; but possible, he gravely added; and I believe it would have been possible to him, with his pride, and his high sense of honour, only Providence did not choose to put him to the proof.

" I should have been an old maid, for I have always been fond of story-telling or of letter-writing. When I cannot have the one, I turn to the other as a matter of course. Mimi knew all my stories; and having one of her own just then, a story which l could read in her bright eyes and radiant smiles whenever Réné appeared, she did not care so much for an old woman's tales. Not that she knew what ailed her, little simpleton, for Mimi's great charm was to be both shrewd aud naïve, as clever children are, but being very deep in the most interesting chapter of her life about that time, she gave my old faded histories of bygone men and women, and dead loves and sorrows a dull unheeding ear. So, being balked of a listener, I took to a correspondent and wrote off Mimi's story to one of my Paris friends. This was about the time that Mimi's visit to me was drawing to a close, and my friend's answer came on the evening of the very day that Mimi had left me. It was a wonderful answer, and related wonderful things, all concerning Mimi. I read it three times over before I could believe in its truth, and when I was at length convinced and converted, and drove off to the Château de Grandsire, I felt as the good fairy may feel when she gets up into her fiery car yoked with cloudy dragons, in order to

help that charming young prince in de-
livering that dear little captive princess
from the enchanted tower.

" The family had done dinner when
I reached Grandsire. I went up to the
salon at once. I am bound to say that the
Grandsires all looked very dismal. Madame
lay on a couch sunk in the deepest melancholy. I fancy the good lady saw towards
what end matters were drifting with Réné
and Mimi, and had some gloomy antici-
pations concerning the future. Mesdemoiselles sat near their parent, looking irrit-
able and injured, whilst Mimi remained
apart, like a little sinner doing penance.

" She sat on a low chair by the fireside;
its carved oaken back rose high above her
bright head, and as I saw her thus very
straight and still, with her hands folded
on her lap and her eyes sadly downcast, I
thought she looked as quaint and as pretty
as a mediæval figure in an old illu-
minated missal. Poor Mimi! I learned
later that her reception had not been a
cordial one, and that there had even been

a passage of arms concerning her at the
dinner-table between Réné and his sisters.
He sat on the opposite side of the fireplace
watching them jealously, and when I came
in and he courteously gave me up his place,
he availed himself of this to go and sit by
Mimi's side.   Eight angry eyes saw the
act and resented it—silently, of course;
for their owners were making civil
speeches to me all the time.   Mimi's heart
was very full, I suppose, for this kindness
of Réné's made her tears flow.

"'Do not,' he entreated, tenderly,
'do not!' He took her hand in the
fervour of his pleading, and Mimi, check-
ing her tears, looked up in his face with a
wistful smile trembling on her young lips.
How far apart were these two, though
sitting thus side by side and hand in hand!
for between them sat that grim spectre,
poverty, who scares away half the visions
of love in this world. He might guard over
and defend her, he might bid her tears not
flow, he might be tender and kind, but
there his power ended.   Of course if he

had been alone in life he would not have
thought twice about asking Mimi to marry
him; but, as it was, a seal was set on his
lips, a seal which honour towards the
orphan girl must never let him violate by
word or look. Seeing them so handsome, so
fond, and so good, though so sorely tried
and tempted, I felt it was delightful to be
a good fairy, and bid those loving hands
remain clasped for ever, and those bright
eyes weep no more. So I waved my
magic wand, and at once the darkness
broke, and a sunbeam pierced it.

"'Ah! Mimi,' said I, 'it is all very
well to be penitent and so on, but I
wonder what you would do if I came, for
instance, to tell you that you had money
—plenty of money?'

"'Do!' cried Mimi, ardently; 'I
should give it all to Réné, every sou.'
Mimi looked so radiant at the thought
that I waved my magic wand a second
time.

"But you would have to give yourself

along with your money. Réné would never take one without the other.'

" Mimi became very red, not at my words, I do believe, but because Réné, after darting a piercing look at me, had turned back to her, and, still holding her hand, now gazed down in her face as if he would read her very soul. For the first time Mimi guessed that she had a lover as well as a friend. She looked happy, troubled, and frightened.

" Oh ! but I am worth nothing,' she cried, hastily, ' nothing at all, and who knows it better than Réné ?'

" ' Well, you shall be put to the proof, both of you. You had an old cousin, Mimi, who never cared about you, and who disinherited you as well as his other relations by his side ; but unluckily he forgot to sign it, and so the will is no good, and your share, Mimi, is two hundred and fifty thousand francs, and you can marry Réné to-morrow if you like it.'

" I said to-morrow, because it sounded well, made a sort of a full stop to my little period, and rounded it off. Of course such quick work was out of the question. But Mimi did not heed this; all the others had seen at once that I was the bearer of great news; Réné had seen it, his mother and his sisters had seen it; he was or he looked calm, but they were breathless and excited as I thus waved my wand a third time, and brought down two hundred and fifty thousand francs with its descending stroke. Mimi alone, now understanding for the first time that I was not jesting, was bewildered. At length the truth, the reality came home to her.

"'Oh! Réné,' she cried laughing and crying too for joy, 'will you have all that money? Oh! you must, you must.'

"Poor Réné! love and pride had a hard contest in him then; but pride, or rather delicacy, prevailed. He gently dropped Mimi's hand, and said kindly, but very gravely :

"'I am glad you have got that money, Mimi.'

"'Oh! but you will have it, too; you

must, Réné, you must,' she said, eagerly.

"Réné did not answer. He could not bear to take the rich girl after having forborne to sue the poor one. Mimi looked very blank and disconsolate. A girl's fancy takes little time to build up a palace of delight, and Heaven alone knows how high love and money had already reared Mimi's castle, when Réné's silence laid the airy fabric in the dust.

"'Then you do not care for me, after all?' she said, and, burying her face in her hands, she burst into tears of mortification, grief, and shame.

"Réné's pride fled at the sight of her sorrow.

"'Not care for you?' he said, with quick and keen reproach; 'look at me, and say that I do not care for you.'

"He removed one hand from her face, then the other, and Mimi, after giving him a quick, shy look, gazed at the fire, and smiled to herself a bright happy smile.

"'Oh! Mimi,' I could not help saying, 'he has liked you all along; did you never find it out?'

"Mimi murmured something, which meant that she had never suspected such a thing, upon which Madame de Grand-sire hysterically declared she had seen it long ago, and her three daughters, with three happy and significant smiles, said they had seen it too. They were too honest, however, to aver that they had liked it; but Mimi, who, if she was mis-chievous, was forgiving, looked at them without one particle of resentment in her soft dark eyes. If her money, potent as charity, covered all her sins, their share of Réné's blood, and their evident, though not disinterested, joy at her good fortune, more than atoned in Mimi's eyes for the unkindness of the past.

"When the good fairy has done her work, viz., blessed the prince and prin-cess, she gets up into her fiery car and vanishes, to appear no more unless at the christening of the first baby, but I was not enough of a fairy to be so disinterested. I stayed the whole of that evening, feast-ing my eyes with the sight of two happy faces. I left late, and reluctantly, and came early the next morning.

"It was a bright spring morning; spring softness was in the air; the trees looked ready to burst into leaf, the birds into song, and Mimi, who stood bare-headed on the perron, looked as fresh and as fair as any flower of spring. I asked how she was. Oh! very well, replied Mimi, only she could not believe it. Of course not, I rejoined; such unexpected good fortune as two hundred and fifty thousand francs was no daily occurrence.

"'Oh! of course, the money is all right,' said Mimi, rather superciliously, and already taking her inheritance as a settled thing; 'but I mean about Réné. Some people are liked because they are good, and I,' added Mimi, looking very rueful, 'have been liked for being naughty; I mean about Mademoiselle Jerôme, you know.'

"She shook her head, and tried to look penitent. Some sort of remorse she, no doubt, felt, for she resumed, confidentially:

'Not that I meant to part them; oh no, certainly not! but you see I shall never tell Réné. I was desperately jealous of her; oh! so jealous.'

"'What, Mimi!' I exclaimed, 'were you in love with Réné, then?'

"'In love!' echoed Mimi, looking greatly offended. 'No indeed, Comtesse. I never thought of such a thing, never. But I was jealous of him. Oh! so jealous. Only he must never know it.'

"'As if he had not known it all along,' gently said Réné's voice behind her.

"And Mimi, turning round with a blushing, startled face, saw Réné, as I had seen him all the time standing in the gloom of the porch. Well, I suppose he had seen it all along, and that was the secret of his tender indulgence towards the little sinner, an indulgence which led him so far, and soon buried the remembrance of Mimi's sin in love."

And, now, need I tell you that the château has been repaired, that the garden

is bright with flowers, that the land yields
such harvests as were never had out of
Goshen, that Mesdemoiselles de Grandsire
are married, and that Réné and Mimi are
as fond and as happy as the prince and
princess of a fairy tale?

My Brother Leonard.

T has always seemed to me, since I passed those giddy but happy years of youth when we feel too much to care to think—it has, I say, always seemed to me, that some of us are born to act and to suffer, and others to sit passively and look on. From childhood upwards to this present hour—when I sit writing alone, a white-haired woman, in an old château of Provence—to be the silent witness of my brother Leonard's life has been my lot. No lover ever came to me; no dream of love ever crossed my

path. But I do not regret it; no, I do not regret it, though I am now a childless old maid, pale and withered. If love, with its blessings and its torments, had sought me, if a husband had taken me to another home than this, what should I have known of that shy and noble heart which grief never conquered, but a great joy broke and stilled for ever!

According to the world's estimate my brother Leonard's life was not an eventful one. For in this, too, the parts allotted to the actors in the great drama of life are unequally divided. Some get the glorious destinies. Their star sets or rises in a sort of tempestuous splendour, and leaves a long track of light behind it through the dull pages of history. So far as I can see, they are not more noble, more heroic, more beautiful than others of whom there is no record, who live and die unremembered save by a few faithful hearts. But, after all, what matter? What is it to my brother Leonard in his grave if the world never knew that it lost in him a pure heart, chivalrous and true as that which once beat in the bosom of Bayard—of the knight who knew neither reproach nor fear, and who died in all honour after living without a stain? My brother Leonard never wielded lance or sword, but there are other battles fought in life than those in which blood is shed; and of all who ever struggled nobly against adverse fate, who knew how to bear defeat, or, harder still, how not to triumph over a conquered enemy, none were ever more worthy of honour than this unremembered man.

He was the eldest and I the youngest of a large family of children, all born in this old Provençal nest built on a rock above the Mediterranean Sea. It is a fair old manor enough, at least I think it so: I like its yellow sunburnt front and the square tower which rises above its low roof, and its many tall windows, with small glass panes, which flash again in the fiery light of the setting sun. I like its broad view of an azure sea with a whitening horizon, and even the arid plains which surround our old home I like too. For in that desert our green garden is like a beautiful oasis, cool and shady. It is an old-fashioned garden—they have none such now—with straight alleys and clipped trees; here and there a few heathen statues, moss-stained and mildewed, appear in the bowers; and on the lawn, in front of the house, a slender fountain ever throws up its waters, howsoever hot the noon-day sun may be. But why do I speak of all this? I am the last of the De Lansacs, and in my languid veins their once hot Provençal blood is dying away feebly.

We were great and rich once, say the records of Provence; but the religious wars proved our undoing. We were Catholics, and had many a fight with our old foes and neighbours the De Sainte Foys, who held the new faith. We beat them of course, but though we were fierce and revengeful, we scorned to enrich ourselves with the spoils of our enemies, and as they soon bent to the storm the warfare which well-nigh ruined us left them rich. Better times came for them, and worse times for us; they married heiresses and throve, whilst we wedded poor girls, had large families, and got poorer and poorer. We had but a slender pittance left under the First Napoleon's reign, but we hated the De Sainte Foys, whose grand old château on the opposite hill went on adding wings and building "pavillons," whilst our poor old manor crumbled away. The sight of it fed our hate. As a child I looked at it with wrath, and even now, when it holds all that is dearest to me, I never care to gaze at its broad façade.

My brother Leonard and I were the only survivors of a large family, and many years divided us. Both our parents were dead, and we lived here alone with a maiden aunt, a pale faded woman, such as I am now, who glided noiselessly about the old rooms and seldom spoke.

All the De Sainte Foys were handsome,

and all the De Lansacs were tall. My brother was six feet high, a gaunt, thin young man, with harsh features, keen eyes, and heavy eyebrows. He was a great sportsman, yet most inconsistently tender-hearted. I never saw him strike his dogs, I never saw him hurt a fly; once his gun was out of his hands he was the gentlest of creatures. For all that he was a great hater. Especially did he hate the Corsican, as he called Bonaparte, and perhaps he hated him all the more that the De Sainte Foys were devoted to the new dynasty, and spent all their time in Paris. I remember the scornful looks my brother often cast on the closed windows of their château. " Just like them," he muttered. " Time-servers; anything for money, anything for rank; just like them!"

I was sent to a convent when I was ten years old, and I remained there till I was seventeen. The nuns were very kind to me, but spite their kindness I pined for my old home and the sea dashing up to the beach, and the green garden with its mutilated statues and its little fountain. So, when I stepped out of the convent-gates into the little carriole which had been sent for me with our old servant Saint Jean, I was, spite a few tears shed at parting from my kind companions, as gay as a lark. The sun was setting when we reached home. The sunburnt land looked flooded with fire and gold, and our old manor seemed almost fresh and young again in the glorious light. I skipped lightly out of the little jolting car; I ran up the stone steps, still as worn and uneven as of yore; I entered the bare old hall with all the grim De Lansacs looking down at me from the walls—we were not a handsome family—and I felt the happiest creature alive, till my aunt, coming downstairs to meet me, told me that Leonard was away in Paris, and that no one knew when he would come back. This sobered me at once. I felt anxious. The times were troubled. Napoleon had left Elba and been conquered at Waterloo. Monsieur de Sainte Foy, I knew, was a proscribed man, for we had met a party of soldiers in search of him. Yet, surely—surely, my brother the Corsican-hater was safe! "Oh yes, quite safe," answered my aunt. Then, looking at me wistfully, she added, "Rose,"—oh! what a mockery that name of mine seems now,—"we have a guest! Our old cousin the Viscount died, you know, leaving a widow and child almost destitute; they are both here, and are likely to remain. You will do well to be friendly with them. Madame de Lansac is a great beauty, and has been rather spoiled, and her little girl is very wilful; but still," said my aunt, looking at me in that wistful way, "you will do well to be friendly with them." Youth is inclined to friendliness, and as my aunt's real meaning never once occurred to me, I cheerfully promised to be all that the beautiful Madame de Lansac could wish. I had no immediate opportunity of showing her how amiable I was; she did not appear, and when my aunt left me to attend to some domestic matters I remained alone.

But does solitude really exist for youth with the delightful companionship of its thousand dreams and hopes and wishes, which are ever flitting about it like gay motes in the noonday sun? Besides, could I feel lonely in the home of my childhood? I went up to my old room, and found it unchanged after all those years: then I ran down to the garden, so fresh and dewy in the pleasant evening; I explored every green nook, I looked fondly at the poor old statues and fancied that they looked back kindly at me. I was half crazy with the joy of being home again.

Of all the rooms in the manor, there was one which, even as a child, I had dearly liked—the upper room in the square turret, whence there was a view of land and sea unrivalled in the province, it was said. Why should I not climb up to it now, like the Lady of Malbrouk in the ballad, and gaze at a blue sea and a pale sky, where white stars began to twinkle, though the horizon was still rosy with departed fires! Perhaps I might see a boat gliding along the waters—one of those low boats with broad lateen sails which I had so often thought of in my inland convent home.

There is a broad central staircase in our manor, with steps of massive stone and balustrades of iron, which takes us to the highest floor of the house, and ends in a long corridor, full of doors, all leading to untenanted chambers save one, which gives access to the dark and narrow spiral stairs that climb up the body of the square tower, and take one to a little room with four windows and a terrace around it. I seldom go there now, for my breath has failed me of late; my sight, too, is weak and dim, and sees no more as it once beheld them the glories of God's world; but I was light as a bird then, aye, and as keen-eyed too, and in a few minutes I had reached the room in the tower. It was much altered from my childish re-membrance of it. I had ever known it bleak and bare-looking, and now it bore manifest signs of being tenanted. There was a flask of wine on the table, and when I curiously lifted up an old piece of tapestry which divided the room in two, I saw with surprise a low camp-bed behind it. " I suppose some servant sleeps here," I thought, and stepping out through one of the windows on the terrace I looked around me with a delight which made me forget all else. The evening was very bright and clear, the sea lay calm and lovely beneath me, and far as eye could reach there spread a noble land stretching to the base of purple-looking hills. It was very fine, but I had no time to linger over the beauty around me. I was roused by a sound of voices coming from the room within. Hiding behind the shutters of the open window, I listened and peeped in.

" I tell you, I cannot," said a man's voice, "and I never said that I could. You must marry him."

The low weeping of a woman answered him. I saw the man first. He was no servant, as I had thought, but a gentleman, and, though long past youth, one of the handsomest men I had ever seen. He stood facing me with his arms folded across his breast, and a careless, defiant look in his dark eyes, that gazed steadily on the clear evening sky. The lady was leaning against the wall with one of her hands resting on a chair. I could not see her at first, but when she turned her face to me I was bewildered at her beauty. He was handsome, but enchanting loveliness are the only words that can describe her. If such she looked to me when overpowered by sorrow, what must she have been when gladness beamed from those deep blue eyes, and happy smiles played on that sweet young face with its cloud of golden hair! I had never seen two such handsome creatures out of the fairy tales, and I was all amazement to see them here.

"O heavens!" she cried, clasping her white hands in an agony of grief, "have I betrayed him for that?"

"Why need he know it?" asked her companion, drawing towards her. I was very young, very innocent, and could not understand their meaning; but some revelation of it came to me when the door of the turret-chamber, which had remained ajar, opened, and my brother Leonard came in with such a look on his white face as I had never seen there before. She uttered a low cry, and starting back he turned pale as death; but Leonard raised his hand, and uttered an imperious " Hush !" which silenced them. For a moment the room was so still that I could hear the low dash of the water on the shore below.

" So that is the end," said Leonard, looking at them in sorrow and in scorn; " that is the end of trust and faith in man and woman. Do not answer—hear me both. Madam, I shall deal first with you. As the widow of my cousin, you asked me for a home, and I gave you one. When you came to this house with your child, your beauty, I confess it, touched my heart; but if you had not one day given me to understand that you had seen

my love, and that it might be welcome, I
never should have wooed a lady so young
and so beautiful as you are. On such a
hint, however, I spoke, and was accepted.
I promised to become your protector and
the father of your child, and you, I suppose, agreed to be true to me. How have
you kept your pledge? Speak; but no,
do not answer; be silent, let not at least
your lips be perjured, even though your
heart is false." He ceased: he was dreadfully agitated, and the lady sobbed pitifully; but he soon recovered, and turning
to her companion, he said, almost
calmly :—

"You, Monsieur de Sainte Foy, came
to me in your peril, and trusting to my
generosity and honour bade me revenge
the old feud of our ancestors by saving
your life. How did I receive you? Like
a brother. And how have you repaid me ?
You know on what errand I went to Paris.
Well, sir, I have succeeded; you are
pardoned. You can leave this house;
you need its shelter no more. You can

go back openly to your own home, where
you, too, have a child, sir, a boy for
whose sake you implored my compassion ;
but mark my words, do not forget to take
this lady with you."

" I cannot—I am married," sulkily said
Monsieur de Sainte Foy, for the first time
attempting to answer my brother.

"You are a widower, sir," answered
Leonard, gravely ; "your wife died whilst
I was in Paris. I repeat it, you can take
this lady with you. And, sir," he added,
his eyes flashing angrily from beneath his
heavy eyebrows, " let me advise you to do
her justice. She is the widow of my
cousin, and I will not see her wronged.
I say no more ; you are my guest, and
though you have forgotten it, sir, I remember it still."

So saying, he turned away and left
them. My eyes were blind with tears,
and my heart was full of sorrow for my
brother Leonard. I stood awhile looking
down at the swelling bosom of the sea ;
then, when I was, or at least looked calm,

I entered the room. The guilty pair had vanished: they left the manor that night, and this was the story of my brother's youth.

From that day forth Leonard was an altered man. He took to books, and became a great reader. His gun was added to the rusty old armour in the hall, and remained there unused; his days were spent in the library. His two hounds, Capitaine and Diane, used to go and seek him there, looking at him with wistful questioning eyes; but though they always got a caress and a kind word, they could not lure him forth. " Why should I go and murder poor harmless creatures that never wronged or betrayed me ?" he once said, and that was the only allusion I ever heard him make to the treachery that had darkened his existence. The blessing of a long life was not granted to the betrayers. Both died within a year of their marriage. Young De Sainte Foy was brought up in Paris, and seldom came to Provence; his stepmother's child was adopted by a distant relation of her mother, and taken to Tours: she, too, married and died young; we never saw her. And thus time passed, and I became a sedate old maid, and after my aunt's death kept house for my brother Leonard, a hale and vigorous old man, whose locks were grey indeed, but whose step was as firm and whose eyes were as keen as ever. He was cheerful, too, and the joyous heartiness of his laugh was something to remember in a man of his years. We left home rarely, and the last time that business took us forth our return was made memorable by a very unforeseen event. We had been a week away, and I felt heartily glad when I saw once more the square tower rising above the yellow front of our old manor. Leonard, too, uttered a relieved " Ah!" as he helped me to alight, and Geneviève, our trusty old female servant, who came forth to meet us with a beaming face.

" Thank Heaven!" she said, crossing herself, " it had seemed a hundred years since we had gone away, but all was right now, and the little girl had come quite safely, praised be Heaven! A real cherub! For though her grandmother had been foolish and wicked enough to marry a De Sainte Foy, the child—glory be to all the saints!—did not belong to that brood."

Here was news for us! The relations of that poor little orphan, our sixth or seventh cousin, had with rare coolness transferred her to us, and taken advantage of our absence to deceive poor Geneviève. Without uttering a word my brother opened the door of our sitting-room. It is a large room, with brown oaken walls and a polished floor. A stream of red sunshine from the west was pouring in through the farthest window, that at which I always sit, because it has a deep recess and a broad ledge on which I put my work. To this ledge the little stranger had climbed, and there she now sat in a forlorn attitude, with her feet gathered beneath her, and her little hands clasped round her knees. She might be six or seven years old. She looked fair as a

lily in her deep mourning, and when she
turned towards us, and shook back her
yellow curls to look at us with wistful
wonder in her deep blue eyes, I knew at
once the lovely face of her beautiful grandmother. I looked at my brother Leonard.
His heavy brows were bent, and his keen
eyes fastened on the child with a steady
gaze. He smiled, too, rather a grim
ironical smile, which seemed to say, " So
the traitress has come back to De Lansac
after all." But the little thing returned
his look very fearlessly, and, to my surprise, smiled up in his face, and never
minded me.

We had not the heart to send her away.
We kept her, and I soon loved her dearly.
She was a good, lovely, and joyous creature. It was like having a bird, or a
sunbeam, or anything bright and gay, to
have her in the house. Leonard never
took the least notice of her; I sometimes
fancied he did not see her, so unconscious
did he seem of her presence. Yet of us
two it was this cold and careless cousin

whom the perverse child preferred. She would leave me any day to sneak after him. Lucie had been a year with us when Geneviève, who doted upon her, came in one afternoon with startled looks. The child was missing; she had been searched for over all the manor, and she was not to be found. My brother looked up from his book, and rose. I followed him up the central stairs, then up again in the tower to the chamber, which he unlocked, and there we found Lucie fast asleep in his chair, curled round like a faithful little spaniel waiting for its master.

My brother never said a word, but took her up, and carried her downstairs still fast asleep, and when Lucie woke below she was on his knee, in his arms, and from that day forth in his heart. They were seldom apart. If you heard my brother's stately step about the house, you also heard a pair of little feet pattering after him. His loud cheerful laugh was ever echoed by a childish voice clear as a silver bell, and if he locked himself up in the library for an hour's lonely reading, his case was vain unless he closed the window; for Lucie would climb up to the sill, jump down, and stealing behind his chair lay her rosy cheek to his, and mingle her golden locks with his iron-grey curls. How could he help loving a creature so endearing—one who thought, felt, loved, and hated as he did, and who detested the De Sainte Foys as cordially as if she had been a genuine De Lansac? I tried to check the feeling: in the first place because it was unchristian, and in the second because the De Sainte Foys were in the shade just then. The son of my brother's betrayer lived in Paris, and squandered or gambled all his large property away. The old château itself would have gone if he had not died rather suddenly, leaving but one son, a young man of whom report spoke well, and who, after his father's death, came to Provence with the intention, it was said, of remaining. It seemed strange to see the windows of the château open again after they had been closed so many years; but we got used to it.

Monsieur de Sainte Foy had not been back more than a month, and Lucie was about seventeen, when he unexpectedly called upon us one morning. I was work-ing, Lucie sat by me unwinding silk, and my brother was reading, when our solitary man-servant Jacques came in, and with scared looks announced our unexpected visitor. We all rose to receive the here-ditary enemy of our house. He was a very handsome young man—all the De Sainte Foys were handsome—with a manly young face, in which I did my best to read hereditary perfidy, but could not. There was truth in his dark eyes, truth in his smile, and truth in the very sound of his voice.

" Monsieur de Lansac," he said, coming forward, " our ancestors have not been friends, I am told; but I am young, I feel guiltless of the past, whatever it may be, and have no wish to cherish its re-sentments or its hatreds. I therefore come to you hoping that you will be so good as to·grant your neighbourly advice and friendliness to one who, though a stranger to this place, means to live and die in the home of those who have gone before him."

My brother smiled very kindly, and held out his hand, and thus a league of amity was struck between the last of the De Lansacs and the last of the De Sainte Foys.

I had always deplored the old feud, but I had my fears about this reconciliation; and when young De Sainte Foy, who did much need my brother's advice, became a frequent visitor at our house, I plainly told those fears to Leonard. Lucie was very lovely and very young. What if this young gentleman should be smitten with her, and win her heart! "Well, and if they should love where would be the harm?" he replied, very kindly.

Ah! what changes time can bring in its train! My brother actually wished for this thing; and when months passed, and no sign of it appeared, I read disappointment in his looks. Well, I too was disappointed. They were both young, both handsome, both gifted and good, and both exactly suited to each other, as it seemed to me. I could not imagine how they met without pleasure and parted without pain, as unconcerned as if the magic of the word " Love" did not exist for them. Besides, I longed for a love-story. There had been none in my own life; my brother's had ended in bitterness. Why would not these perverse young things give me one ? It would have been so pleasant to see them adoring each other, quarrelling and making it up again, and going through their pretty idyll in the green garden of our old manor. I was sorry that they did not care for each other, and I could not help saying so to my brother one evening as we walked alone in the garden. Lucie was up in the tower; she had taken a great fancy to it of late, and went up to it every evening.

" And I, too, am sorry," replied Leonard, shaking his grey locks regretfully; " for, Rose, I like that young man very dearly; strange that a De Lansac should say so, is it not? But he does not care for the child, and love will be free. Where is she? In the tower, as usual. Let us go up to her. It feels close down here."

I do not know why I opposed Leonard's wish. I seemed to have a presentiment of coming evil, and yet all I thought of was that the stairs were steep and high, and that the exertion would be too much for my brother. But he only laughed, and said he would go and see what stars the child was reading up there. He was soon tired, as I had foreseen, and obliged to rest on the dark stairs of the tower. A sound of voices from above came down to us. Lucie, if she was there, was not alone. I heard my brother breathing heavily.

" Leonard," I whispered, " let me go," for it was a man's voice that mingled with hers.

VOL. II.   X

He did not answer, but he put me by; in a moment, as it seemed, he had reached the door and pushed it open. I followed him in. Lucie was alone in the room. Without looking at her, my brother went straight to the window, and said calmly, " You may come in, sir."

And thus summoned, young Monsieur de Sainte Foy left the balcony and entered the room. I looked at them both. There they were—the two ingrates—as I had seen them so many years before : beautiful and deceiving, again betraying the kind friend and the generous enemy; but they were younger than in those bygone days, and I could read shame and grief on their two faces. My brother looked at them with the very look which I remembered— a cold and angry look; and he said, in a cold hard voice :—

" I have read somewhere that what has been is ; that the same men and women live again and again to do the same deeds over and over, and I find the truth of it this day. You, Monsieur de Sainte Foy,

came to me, your hereditary enemy, asking our old animosity to be forgotten ; and
when I opened my house to you, as if you
had been one of its sons, you abused my
hospitality. Even so did your grandfather
act, sir, when I saved his life many years
ago. Hush! you will speak presently.
You," he added, turning to Lucie, "have
betrayed me, your adopted father, as she
whose image you are betrayed me, her
future husband ; and, true to your destiny,
you chose to do so with the descendant of
the man to whom I was sacrificed. I, too,
fulfilled my part in this repetition of an
old story, for I was blind, trusting, and
easily deceived. Well, as I acted before
I shall act again. Let the lot you have
chosen be your lot. You want this young
girl, Monsieur de Sainte Foy ? Take her!
For the sake of the few drops of De
Lansac blood which flow in her veins she
may remain in this house till she becomes
your wife ; but I shall thank you both to
have the wedding over quickly, and then
let me see either of you no more."

Lucie buried her face in her hands, and sobbed pitifully; but the young man became crimson, and said passionately,

"You wrong us, sir; we have been imprudent, but treachery was not in our thoughts. I repeat it, you wrong us."

"Do you think I am angry?" replied my brother Leonard. "Why, you could not help yourselves. It was in your blood to betray me, and it was my lot to be deceived by you."

"Ah! do not say so," cried Lucie, attempting to detain him as he turned to the door; but he who had so loved her looked at her so coldly that she shrank back afraid. So we left them; and, turning back, I saw her sinking on a chair, pale as death, whilst her lover stood looking after my brother, gnawing his nether lip, as if he still smarted under the sting of those bitter words: "It was in your blood to betray me."

Sad and bitter were the days that followed this ill-fated evening. I attempted to say a few words for poor Lucie, but my brother's only answer was, " Keep her out of my sight till they are married."

He was a wilful man—one, too, whom the memory of a great wrong had em‑ bittered. It was useless to dispute his commands, and I told Lucie so.

" I have deserved it," was her only answer; and she submitted, and kept out of his way.

The wedding was to be a speedy one, according to my brother's wish; but, oh! how joyless were the few preparations, and with how heavy a heart I made them! Three days before that appointed for the marriage I again tried to move Leonard. It was a clear and calm evening, and we sat together on the wooden bench in the bower where the dilapidated Pan is ever playing on a broken reed. I pleaded for the two culprits. I spoke of their youth, of the wish he had felt for their union, of forgiveness and indulgence. He heard me out, then said :—

" I trusted them, and they deceived me without need, without cause. By what magic can I ever trust them again?"

I felt silenced. What is there, indeed, that can restore a lost faith? Still, I was seeking for some argument wherewith to move him, when we were both startled by a sound of steps on the gravelled path. Lucie and young De Sainte Foy stood before us. My brother's pale thin face took a slight hectic tinge, and he looked angrily at them both, but said not one word.

" Monsieur de Lansac," said the young man—and I had never seen a nobler and a more loyal look on man's face than I then saw on his—" we would not thus intrude upon you if we could help doing so, but we cannot; be so good, therefore, as to bear with us for a few moments."

" Speak," impatiently said my brother.

" All we have to say is this : our love was born and ripened in ignorance; our interviews were the result of accident; we never designed to deceive you, or to betray your trust, and you have laid upon us the burden of a sin and shame which, however much appearances may condemn us, we will not bear. We love each other very dearly, but having no other means to convince you, we have resolved to part for ever rather than give you the right to think that we, the descendants of two who unhappily wronged you, have combined to betray you in your old age as you were betrayed by them in your youth. In your presence, therefore, and with her full consent, I give up all claim to this young lady's love. Here I bid her adieu for ever, and let the bitterness of such a parting atone for the imprudence which has cost us both so dear."

I looked at Leonard; I could scarcely see him, my eyes were so dim with tears; but he replied, in a low, bitter voice—

" Yes, the old man has but a few years to live. It will do to wait till he is in his grave, will it not ?"

" Ah ! we have not deserved this !" cried Lucie.

" No, we have not deserved it," answered her lover. " Sir, you wrong us very much indeed. A thought so cruel as that of waiting for your death never came to us. Our parting is to be irrevocable. My house and land are to be sold, and the first vessel which leaves Marseilles will take me to India. We may never meet again, and if we do, years will have passed over us—years and their changes. If you do not trust us, if you think we are acting a part and speculating on your grave, the sin be yours, not ours."

"Marvellous!" replied my brother Leonard, with a low, ironical laugh. "A young man gives up his mistress, a girl gives up her lover, and all for the sake of a grey-headed old man! Do not ask me to believe it."

"Sir, it is not merely for your sake that we part," said young De Sainte Foy, with an angry light in his dark eye; "it is also for the sake of our honour. Our error has sullied it, but our sacrifice shall redeem it: and you yourself, sir, you our accuser, shall confess it."

My brother was staggered, but he would not relent.

"Yes—yes, I know," he said, impatiently; "you think I am one of those soft-hearted stage fathers, who forgive the sinners and bestow their blessing in the last act. You are mistaken. If Lucie gives you up, she must give you up entirely. Do you hear, both of you—entirely? I ask for no sacrifice; I expect none. But if you do give up this thing for the sake of your honour, you must not look back."

"We mean it so," answered the young man, in a low tone. "Lucie." He turned to her. She twined her arms around his neck; for a few moments they stood before us in the pale moonlight, clasped in so passionate an embrace that it seemed as if they could never again be sundered. Neither spoke, neither wept; but when I looked at them—so young, so fond, so noble, and so handsome—and thought that they were to part, I could not restrain my tears. My brother looked on unmoved, and uttered not a word of relenting. Young Monsieur de Sainte

Foy at length put her by, and walked away without bidding us adieu. She stood looking after him, pale and tearless.

"Lucie," quietly said my brother, "you may call him back, if you repent your choice."

She looked at him swiftly, with a vague hope, poor child; but there was no relenting in my brother's eye, so her face fell a little, and she only shook her head, as much as to say, "I do not repent."

I have often wondered how my dear brother, so generous, so kind, could be so hard to these two. But he had trusted them entirely, and it pierced his very heart that they should have deceived him. Indeed, there was no reason why they should have done so. It must have been the waywardness of youth which allured them into this needless secrecy, giving sweetness to a hidden love. I could have made all these allowances for them, it seemed to me; but Leonard could not. He was hard because he was himself the soul of truth and honour, and he was un-

relenting because the memory of his old
wrong had never left him. It may also
be, that in his secret heart he thought to
try the two culprits for a time, and forgive them in the end; but it was not to be.

Lucie bore this great trial with quiet
fortitude. She looked pale, and her
old joyousness was gone; but if she
grieved or wept, she kept both tears and
sorrows to herself. To my brother she
was as gentle and affectionate as ever.
His manner to her was unaltered, save for
a slight shade—a very slight shade—of
more tenderness. I think my heart must
have been young still in those days, for I
kept on hoping to the last. I used to
watch my brother Leonard's face, trying
to read signs of pity or forgiveness in his
harsh features, but I saw them not.
Then, I confess it, I acted a little part. I
would sigh deeply within his hearing, or
look persistently at the château of the
Sainte Foys, when we were all in the garden, or murmur a " Poor child !" whenever Lucie left the room; but my brother

would not see, he would not hear—he never questioned me, or gave me the opportunity I wanted. At length I got desperate, and spoke to him one evening.

"Leonard," I said, "will you not relent? Do you know that young De Sainte Foy's house and land are for sale, and will go to the highest bidder? Do you know that he sails for India to-morrow on board the 'Memphis?'"

"You have seen him," said Leonard, knitting his heavy eyebrows, "and he has asked you to say all this to me?"

"I have seen him, but not spoken to him," I replied, a little angrily. "He is the shadow of his former self—so pale, so worn, so sad, has he grown at all this. Do not let him go, Leonard,"

"He will come back when I am in my grave," answered Leonard, moodily. It was useless to argue. Mistrust had taken an iron grasp of him, and would not let him go again.

On the evening of the following day we missed Lucie. Geneviève told us that Mademoiselle had gone up to the tower; I guessed what had taken her there, but Leonard did not seem to think that she might wish for solitude, for he said to me "Let us go to her."

Never shall I forget the sight that met us as we entered that ill-fated room. It was full of a broad ruddy glow which came from the sea, lighting up the coast for miles around; a vessel was on fire! My heart seemed to stand still in the horror of that moment, and yet how I remember the pale evening sky, with the round white moon, and Lucie's ghastly face and wild eyes, as she stood gazing on the cruel sight in mute despair!

My brother stared at the burning vessel. "God forgive me, miserable sinner!" he cried—"God forgive me!" And he sank back with a groan, and would have fallen but for me.

He never recovered the blow; for it was the 'Memphis' whose destruction we thus witnessed, and young De Saiute Foy, who had sailed in her, was not amongst the few who escaped to tell her lamentable history. He was the last of his name, and with him ended the line of our hereditary enemies.

And Leonard, as I said, never recovered that blow. His vigorous old age gave place to decrepitude; his grey hairs grew white, his form was bent, his steps became feeble and unsteady. The knowledge that his mistrust and hardness had doomed that brave and true young man to a cruel death, and condemned Lucie, his darling, to go through the agony of such a grief, was more than he could bear. He brooded over the thought incessantly.

The weather was fine, and that part of the garden where he could sit and look at the château of the De Sainte Foys, now closed for ever on its ancient tenants, was that which he liked best. He would sit there, gazing at the shut-up mansion, for hours at a time. When I tried to rouse him from this bitter contemplation, he only shook his head and said : " It was an old quarrel; it lasted ages, but the De Sainte Foys had the best of it in the long

run, Rose. Far better perish on board
the burning ' Memphis'—better lose love
and life for honour, than live to be a hard
and revengeful old man." This was the
thought that was killing him. " Make
him forget," said the doctor whom I called
in, " and then you may hope to save him."

Make him forget! I would have laid
down my life for it—oh, how gladly !—but
it passed my power ; Lucie, herself, did her
best and failed. What she really felt and
suffered she never showed. She was a
generous little creature, and from the first
she buried her grief deep in her heart,
and kept it there fast locked from our view.
Her one thought seemed to be to cling to
Leonard. He no longer read now, though
when he could not go to the garden to
look at the château of the De Sainte Foys
he would sit in the library with a book
lying unread before him, his moody eyes
ever seeming to gaze on the tragic ending
of the ill-fated ' Memphis.' But no more
then than formerly could he escape Lucie.
She would steal in upon him as she had so

often stolen in her childhood, and lay her cheek to his fondly and silently. I do believe that she had never loved him more tenderly than she did then, perhaps because of the same deep grief through which they both suffered, and which, as I saw with an aching heart, was wasting them both away. This had lasted three weeks—weeks long as years—when the end came. We were all sitting in the garden, I remember, in that very arbour where the poor god Pan is ever piping away, when Geneviève came up to us with startled looks.

" Monsieur !—Mademoiselle !" she gasped. " He is alive !—here he is !"

My brother rose as with an electric shock. He strode towards her ; he pushed her away, and then young De Sainte Foy stood living before us. " Sir," he said, " I did not mean to intrude upon you ; but my life has been saved by a miracle, and as I am told that the report of my death has been a heavy trouble to you, I come——"

He did not go on.

" Thank God !" gasped my brother. " Thank God ! But it is too much ; ah ! it is too much."

And it was too much indeed ! The joy was too exquisite and too great for his true heart, for as he uttered the words he sank back on his seat and died. What sorrow, what faith betrayed, and love lost, had not done, the joy of seeing his hereditary foe safe and well before him, did.

My little tale is told. I am very happy, for my dearest Leonard has only gone before, and the two whom we both loved so dearly are blest. Yes, I am happy; but you know now what I meant when I said that the lot of some is to suffer, and that of others to look on. This was certainly my lot, and maybe that is why, though so happy, I sometimes feel rather useless. My part is ended, and all I can do now is to remember what I can see no more. Be it so ; memory, too, is sweet.

END OF THE SECOND VOLUME.

LONDON:

Printed by A. Schulze, 13, Poland Street.   (R T.)

CPSIA information can be obtained
at www.ICGtesting.com
Printed in the USA
BVHW071701061118
532319BV00011B/861/P

9 780483 287716